Mary Anne's Book

**Other books by
Ann M. Martin**

*Rachel Parker, Kindergarten Show-off
Eleven Kids, One Summer
Ma and Pa Dracula
Yours Turly, Shirley
Ten Kids, No Pets
Slam Book
Just a Summer Romance
Missing Since Monday
With You and Without You
Me and Katie (the Pest)
Stage Fright
Inside Out
Bummer Summer*

BABY-SITTERS LITTLE SISTER series
THE BABY-SITTERS CLUB mysteries
THE BABY-SITTERS CLUB series

Mary Anne's Book

Ann M. Martin

AN
APPLE
PAPERBACK

SCHOLASTIC INC.
New York Toronto London Auckland Sydney

Interior art and cover drawing by Angelo Tillery

Cover painting by Hodges Soileau

ISBN 0-590-22865-X

12 11 10 9 8 7 6 5 4 3 2 1   6 7 8 9/9 0 1/0

Printed in the U.S.A.   40

First Scholastic printing, March 1996

The author gratefully acknowledges
Jeanne Betancourt
for her help in
preparing this manuscript.

Mary Anne's Book

CHAPTER 1

It was Saturday morning. I was about to roll over and go back to sleep when my kitten Tigger stood on my chest, looked me in the eye, and meowed three times in a row. I knew exactly what he was saying. "Get up or I'll bounce all over this bed. Feed me now." I gave Tigger a gentle push off the bed and said, "You win, Tigger." Then I kicked back the covers and got up.

By the time we entered the kitchen I realized that Tigger and I were the only ones home. My dad and stepmother were already out doing their regular Saturday morning errands. I knew they'd be home soon. But one member of our family wouldn't be coming home for a long time: my stepsister Dawn. Dawn recently moved to California to live with her dad, her brother Jeff, and their new stepmother Carol. Since California is three thousand miles from where I live in Stoneybrook, Connecticut, I don't see Dawn very often. She and I were best friends even before we became sisters. I miss her. I looked at the clock on the microwave. Nine-thirteen. That meant it was only six-thirteen in California. Too early to call Dawn.

I opened a can of yummy chicken parts for Tigger and poured cereal for myself. I would have liked pancakes or french toast, but I didn't want to take the time to cook them. I had a big school assignment to work on and I was determined to finish it over the weekend. The assignment was to write the story of my life so far — my autobiography. It may seem strange for a thirteen-year-old to be working on an autobiography, but all the eighth graders at Stoneybrook Middle School have to write one. We can use photographs and other memorabilia to illustrate our autobiographies, but mostly they're supposed to be written documents.

I couldn't wait to get back to work on it. That's right, I'm one of those people who actually enjoys school and doesn't mind doing homework. Anyone who sees me for the first time can tell that I'm the quiet, studious type. I'm the short, dark-haired girl watching from the sidelines, the one who's dressed conservatively. (My friends say my style is "quiet.")

What else would my friends say about me?

Well, I cry easily. For instance, I cry at movies and over some of the books I read. I cry over personal, real-life situations too, such as my friends' problems. I've also been known to shed a few tears over my own problems. But more about those later.

None of my friends is as shy or weepy as I am, but they don't mind my moods. I have some *great* friends. We're all members of the Baby-sitters Club, a sitting business which was started by my very best friend (and club president), Kristy Thomas. Kristy and I had lived next door to each other since we were babies. That changed when we were in the seventh grade. That year Kristy's mother married Watson Brewer, and her family moved into Watson's house, which happened to be a *mansion*. Then my dad married Dawn's mother, Sharon Schafer. The Schafer house was bigger than ours, so Dad and I moved in with them. Our new home isn't a mansion, but it's special. It's a two-hundred-year-old farm house with low ceilings and doorways, slanted floors, a ghost (according to Dawn), a secret passage (that used to be part of the Underground Railroad), a genuine outhouse (that we don't use), and a great big barn. I love our new old house.

My other friends in the Baby-sitters Club are Claudia, Stacey, Abby, Jessi, Mal, Shannon, and Logan. Claudia Kishi was one of my first friends, and is the BSC vice-president. Claud's only official duty as V.P. is to host our meetings every Monday, Wednesday, and Friday. Her *un*official duty is providing us with the junk food that she keeps hidden in her room. Claudia is a beautiful, tall, Japanese-American. She's a gifted artist and dresses in outrageous clothes. People are always saying, "Wow! What a great outfit!" when they see Claud. Unlike me, she loves the attention. The way Claudia dresses is just one expression of her artistic talent.

Stacey McGill is also very into fashion. Her wardrobe is more sophisticated than funky, though. Stacey says that her sense of fashion comes from growing up in New York City. Her parents are divorced and her dad lives in New York City. So, while Stacey spends most of her time in Stoneybrook and goes to school with us, she also has a bedroom in her dad's New York City apartment. Stacey often feels torn between her parents and has had a lot of problems with the divorce. She also has diabetes, which means she has to be very careful about what she eats (absolutely *no* sweets) and has to give herself insulin shots. As you might guess, this has helped to make Stacey a very responsible person — and a responsible club treasurer. (It also helps that she's a math whiz!)

Dawn, my stepsister, used to be an officer in the BSC. Now that she's living in California she's an honorary member of the club. I miss Dawn so much that I'm getting teary just thinking about her. Dawn is a member of a baby-sitting club in California called the We ♥ Kids Club. My sister is athletic (she loves to surf), full of fun, and is seriously into eating healthy foods. She actually prefers a tofu burger to a hamburger, carrot sticks to french fries, and an apple to an ice-cream cone.

Abby Stevenson is a new member, and the alternate officer, of the BSC. (She fills in for any club officer who can't attend a meeting.) She's the opposite of me in temperament. Abby is extremely outgoing and is always cracking jokes and fooling around. But Abby and I have one important thing in common: we both have lost one of our parents. Abby's father died in a car accident about seven years ago. My mother died when I was a baby. By the way, Abby has a twin sister, Anna, but Anna isn't a member of the BSC.

Logan Bruno is the only male member of the BSC. Actually, he's an associate member, which means we call on him when we have extra baby-sitting jobs that we can't fill with regular members. Logan is a terrific sitter and a terrific guy. He's kind, intelligent, sweet, sensitive, funny, understanding, good-looking, and . . . he's my boyfriend. Logan and I have had our ups and downs. For instance, we once had a big misunderstanding about how much time we were going to spend together. He expected me to spend all my free time with him. But that made me feel suffocated and unhappy. I like my independence. Now we each understand what's important to the other person and our relationship is great. Logan Bruno is one of my very best friends.

Shannon Kilbourne is the other associate member of the club. Since the BSC is only one of Shannon's many extracurricular activities, we don't see her much. Also, she's the only one in our group who goes to a private school instead of Stoneybrook Middle School.

Jessi Ramsey and Mallory Pike, the junior members of the club, are younger than the rest of us. But the only real difference between us and them is that they can't baby-sit at night, unless they are sitting for their own families. Jessi and Mal are responsible, excellent members of the BSC and good friends. Mal is a serious writer and artist who wants to be a children's book author when she grows up. Jessi is an amazing ballet dancer. I'm sure she'll be a professional ballerina someday.

I finished my cereal and was about to go upstairs to work on my autobiography when the doorbell rang. I saw that it was our post-man and opened the door.

"Priority mail for you, Ms. Spier," he said. I took the envelope, thanked him, and went back inside.

I saw right away that the return address was Maynard, Iowa. The package was from my grandmother, Verna Baker. I sat on the stairs and opened it. Inside was a letter and a pink satin baby book.

The letter started with my grandmother's saying that she was happy I was writing my autobiography and that she hoped I would send her a copy when I finished it. She went on to say that she'd recently located my baby book and thought it might be helpful as I worked on my project. "It's hard for me to believe that eleven years have passed since I completed the baby book that your mother began," she wrote.

I put the letter aside to finish later. I couldn't wait to see what my mother had written about me when I was a baby and she was still alive. The first entries — all in her neat handwriting — were straight facts about how much formula I drank (a lot) and when I slept (most of the time). Then I read, "Mary Anne gave me her first genuine smile today. What a beautiful smile. What a beautiful baby." I burst into tears. I wiped my eyes with the back of my sleeve so my tears wouldn't fall on the words my mother had written about me.

"What's happened, Mary Anne?" asked my dad.

"My goodness, what is it?" exclaimed Sharon.

I hadn't heard my dad and stepmother come in through the kitchen. Now they were standing at the foot of the stairs staring at me. Sharon looked terrified. "Are Dawn and Jeff okay?" she asked. "Did you get a call from California?"

"They're okay," I assured her. "I'm sorry I scared you." I put the letter and the baby book back in the envelope. "I'm okay, too."

"What were you reading that made you cry?" my dad asked.

"Just stuff for my autobiography," I replied. "Grandma Baker sent me the baby book she and my mother wrote about me."

I don't usually mention my mother to my father. I know it makes him sad. And I didn't think it was fair to talk about my mother (my father's first wife) in front of Sharon (his second wife). But Sharon didn't seem to mind. She sat next to me on the stairs and took my hand in hers. "I'm sorry you feel sad," she said softly. *That*, of course, made me cry even harder.

"Is your autobiography going to be sad?" my dad asked.

I thought about that for a second, then I smiled through my tears. "No," I answered, "it isn't going to be sad, because my life isn't sad." I looked from Sharon to Dad. "I'm happy and I'm lucky."

"I'm glad to hear you say that," Dad said. "Because you make me feel happy and lucky."

"Me , too," said Sharon. She gave me a soft kiss on the cheek.

My dad cleared his throat in the way he does when he's getting choked up over something. "Well," he said, "I better put the groceries away before the frozen items melt." Putting stuff away is a job my dad loves. He is just about the neatest person in the world. He even alphabetizes cereal boxes and the bottles on the herb and spice rack. "After I put things away I'm going to make ham and french toast for brunch," he told me. "Will you have some?"

"I'd love to," I said. "But can I work on my autobiography while you cook?"

"Sure," he said.

"I'll put the groceries away, Richard," Sharon offered, "so you can start cooking."

My dad and I exchanged a smile. Sharon is as disorganized as my dad is organized. If she put the food away we were apt to find the ice cream melted all over the vegetable bin and the lettuce in the freezer.

I knew Sharon and my dad would figure out who was doing what in the kitchen. And that they'd be happy while they were doing it.

Meanwhile, I went upstairs to work on my autobiography. I grabbed a fresh box of Kleenex from the bathroom cupboard. Even happy things can make me cry.

The Story of My Life,
by Mary Anne Spier

From Birth to Six Years

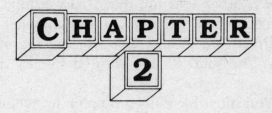

CHAPTER 2

I wish with all my heart that I could remember the first few months of my life. Because if I did, I would remember my mother.

My father told me that I was a quiet and sweet baby. "When we first brought you home I didn't want to leave for work in the mornings," he said. "I just wanted to stay home and look at you."

"You must have been home a lot when my mother was sick," I said.

"Yes," he said, "I was home a great deal then. So it was the three of us, together. Alma, your mother, wanted you near her all the time. Your crib was next to her bed. You were a comfort and a joy to her."

It makes me happy to know that I helped my mother, even if I can't remember. My grandmother Baker — my mother's mother — talks about what a comfort I was to her and to my grandfather, too. After my mother died, Dad was terribly upset and concerned about whether he could take care of an infant on his own. When my mother's parents offered to take care of me, my dad thought that would be best. So he let me go to Iowa to live with my grandparents. They raised me until I was eighteen months old. I don't remember being with my grandparents, but Grandmother Baker has told me about that part of my life. She also continued the baby book my mother began. It's filled with details (most of them pretty boring) about my early life.

My favorite picture of my mother and me.

When I visited my grandmother recently, I asked her what I was like as a baby. "When you first came to us," she told me, "you were clingy. You didn't want us out of your sight, even for a minute." She smiled. "But of course we didn't want to lose sight of you for a minute either, so it worked out fine. Your grandfather would hold you against his shoulder and go off to the fields to look at the corn. And when I went to town, I'd push you around in the stroller while I did my errands. Everyone admired you."

"Didn't it bother you when I cried and stuff?" I asked. I was remembering some fussy infants I'd baby-sat for.

"No," she said. "First of all, you were a very easy baby. And second, we were so glad to have you. For us it was a way of keeping Alma alive."

My earliest memory is of being with my dad. So it must have been when I was living with him again. I remember being in the house on Bradford Court. I was playing on the living room rug with a pile of plastic cones that fit into one another. Someone must have been baby-sitting for me, but I don't remember who. I do remember hearing a car pull into the driveway, which I recognized as the sound I always heard before my father came through the kitchen door. I put down the cones and

Dad and me. This is my first memory.

stood up. When my father entered I was already running toward him. He reached out and lifted me into his arms. It must have been winter, because I remember the cold on his coat and face. I don't remember what we said. I don't even know if I could talk yet. I just remember how glad I was to be with him, and the feel of his cold cheek against my warm one.

From the time I was three or so I have a lot of memories. I remember my father braiding my hair every morning, and sitting at the table to eat breakfast cereal together. My dad liked to play number and letter games with me. On Saturday mornings we would sit side by side on the couch and watch *Sesame Street* reruns. We'd sing the alphabet and numbers songs along with the characters and their guests. My dad thought Letter Man was hysterical. Big Bird was my favorite.

I also enjoyed playing with my Legos while my father worked at his desk in the living room. My dad's a lawyer, so he often brings paperwork home. He says he brought work home on weekends so he wouldn't have to go into the office. He wanted to take care of me as much as he could.

For as long as I can remember we ate out on Sunday evenings. I recently asked him why he bothered bringing a wiggly three-year-old to a restaurant. He said he wanted me to learn early how to behave properly in public. We always went to the same restaurant, sat at the same table, and ordered the same meals. He'd have roast beef with a baked potato. I'd have a hamburger without the roll and mashed potatoes. For dessert he'd have apple pie and I'd have a scoop of chocolate ice cream.

I remember being sad when the weekend ended and my father had to go back to work. I never liked being with the baby-sitters as much as with my dad.

One morning my dad announced, "No baby-sitter this morning. Today you are going to nursery school and I want to take you myself for your first day." He braided my hair especially tightly.

"Ouch," I protested.

"Sorry," he said. "But we want you to look extra nice for nursery school." He reminded me that a few weeks earlier we had visited the school. I vaguely remembered a place where a lot of other kids were playing and having a good time. "Claudia and Kristy are going to nursery school, too," he said.

The first activity on my first day of nursery school was storytime. My dad read to me every night and I liked hearing stories. So far, nursery school was fine. Especially since my dad was sitting on a little chair at the side of the room, watching me.

While we were still in the story circle we sang, "If You're Happy and You Know It." I'd never heard that song before, but I learned it pretty quickly. And my dad was still in that little chair smiling at me.

Next we broke into groups and played in different parts of the room. The teacher told me to go to the dress-up corner with two girls I didn't know. I didn't want to dress up, but I helped the others pick out what to wear, which was fun enough for me. I was arranging a big red feather boa around a girl's shoulders when my dad appeared beside me. He kissed me on the top of the head and said he'd see me later. Then he was gone.

Uh-oh. I wasn't so happy about being in nursery school anymore. I was terrified I'd never see my dad again. What if my father forgot he had left me there? Tears came to my eyes. What if he remembered but forgot the way to the nursery school? Just then I felt a little punch on my arm. "Hi," another kid said. It was Kristy.

She grabbed my hand. "Come on, Mary Anne," she commanded. She pulled me over to the block corner where Claudia was building a high tower. "Nursery school is fun," Claudia said. "Want to help me build a beautiful building?" I nodded. In a few minutes I was so busy handing Claudia blocks that I forgot about crying.

I stuck by Kristy and Claudia during snacktime. When the teacher announced rest period, Kristy unrolled my mat between hers and Claudia's. "These are our permanent rest places," she told me. I didn't know what permanent meant, but I did know that Kristy would look out for me in nursery school. And that being in nursery school with Kristy and Claudia was going to be a lot better than being at home alone with a baby-sitter.

Now that we were in nursery school together, Kristy, Claudia, and I began playing together more outside of school, too. Since Kristy lived next door to me and Claudia lived across the street, it was easy for my sitters to arrange play dates. They were probably thrilled when I went to other kids' houses. That meant they had time off.

My favorite place for us to play was at Claudia's. I thought that, next to my father, Claudia's grandmother, Mimi, was the most wonderful person in the world. "And how are you today, our Mary Anne?" she would ask.

I remember once when I was playing in

Claudia's yard, I fell down and scraped my knee. It was a little scrape that didn't even hurt. But I still let Mimi gather me in her arms and sit me on her lap. "Well, Mary Anne, let's take a look at it." I enjoyed every second of her fussing over me. She brought me inside and cleaned my knee with antiseptic. Then she suggested I rest with her for a few minutes on the back porch. I sat next to Mimi in the rocking chair and we watched Claudia and Kristy kicking a ball around the yard.

After awhile she asked, "Do you want to play again?" I shook my head no, snuggled even closer, and took a deep breath of the flowery smell that was special to Mimi.

When Mimi died not long ago, Claudia gave me one of her grandmother's silk scarves. It still has that wonderful Mimi smell.

Going to kindergarten with Claudia and Kristy was as much fun as nursery school. We were always together. We stayed together in first grade, too. But first grade was not as much fun for me as nursery school and kindergarten. That's because our teacher was Mrs. Frederickson.

Mrs. Frederickson's volume control knob seemed to be permanently stuck on extra loud. She was one of those teachers who never spoke softly, but yelled all day long. Being in

I liked to pretend that mimi was my grandmother, too.

Mrs. Frederickson's class was my first experience with an adult who yelled. I didn't like it.

Mimi picked us up after our first day of first grade. I made sure to hold one of Mimi's hands as we walked home. Claudia held onto the other one. Kristy didn't seem to mind that there wasn't a Mimi hand for her to hold. Her hands were occupied with tossing a rubber ball in the air and catching it.

"And how was first grade?" Mimi asked us as we walked along.

"I don't like it," said Claudia. "The teacher's mean."

"I'm going to wear earmuffs to school," Kristy announced. "She yells."

"What about you, Mary Anne?" asked Mimi. "What do you think of first grade?"

"It's okay," I told Mimi.

She gave my hand a gentle squeeze of approval.

"Maybe your teacher was a little bit nervous on the first day," she suggested.

"She's mean all the time," insisted Claudia. "I know it."

"It's good to think in a positive way, my Claudia," said Mimi.

I decided then that I would never complain about Mrs. Frederickson to Mimi. I wanted her to see that I would always "think in a positive way." I wanted Mimi to love me. Now I know that Mimi would have loved me whether I complained about Mrs. Frederickson or not. Mimi was the kindest, most understanding woman I've ever known. I used to pretend that she was my grandmother.

At dinner that evening my father asked, "So how do you like first grade, honey?"

"I don't like it much," I admitted.

"You don't?" he said. He seemed alarmed. "Why not?"

"There aren't any playtimes. There isn't even a dress-up corner. And no games. The teacher yells all the time. I want to go back to kindergarten. Claudia and Kristy want to go back to kindergarten, too. They said so."

My father put on the serious expression he wore when he was teaching me something such as how to print my name or how to put a napkin on my lap before eating. "Now, Mary Anne," he said, "as you go through school you will find that your teachers all have different teaching styles. They aren't going to change because you don't like the way they act. You are the one who has to adjust. I'm sure Mrs. Frederickson is a fine teacher. And I know you can be a fine student. If you behave and do your work you two will get along fine. I promise you that. Will you do your very best for me?"

I'd do anything for my father, so I promised him I would be a good girl. But I made sure to add, "I still don't like when she yells."

"Just remember," he said, "Mrs. Frederickson is not yelling at you. She's yelling at other kids. The ones who aren't behaving and doing their work."

I remembered how Mrs. Frederickson yelled at Claudia for drawing a picture of a rainbow instead of practicing the letter "A." And how she'd yelled at Kristy for getting into a fight with Alan Gray during recess. "I don't like it when she yells at anybody," I told my dad.

"Just as long as you're a good girl, I'm sure everything will be fine," he said.

I nodded. But I wasn't convinced. So far the only good thing about first grade was that Kristy and Claudia were in my class.

The Tea Party

CHAPTER 3

When I was six I had four very important people in my life: my father, Kristy, Claudia, and Mimi. So I didn't think much about not having a mother. Not until the first grade Mother's Day tea party.

The Tea Party

Even though Mrs. Frederickson was a yeller, I did all right in first grade. I liked the school-work and I especially loved to read. I would have read all the time, if there weren't so many other things I enjoyed doing, such as going to the park with my friends and playing at their houses.

After dinner my dad and I would go into the living room and put music on the tape deck. He would do work he'd brought from the office or read the newspaper, and I would read to myself from my picture books. But when it was time for bed and I was cleaned up and tucked in, my dad would read from a chapter book. That was the best. My favorite chapter book that year was *Anne of Green Gables* by L. M. Montgomery. I understand now that I identified with Anne because she didn't have a mother either.

Sometimes, when Mrs. Frederickson was yelling at the class, I'd think about what had happened in *Anne of Green Gables* the night before. (I wanted to put my hands over my ears, but that just would have given her one more thing to yell about.)

The best thing about being six was living near Kristy and Claudia. Kristy's and my bed-room windows faced one another and with the blinds up we could see into each other's rooms. In warm weather we could talk to each other through the opened windows. Our rooms were so close that sometimes I pretended they were in the same house and that we were sisters.

Claudia had a sister, Janine. Janine was in the third grade and was in charge of Claudia, Kristy, and me when we walked to and from school. Claudia didn't always get along with Janine. They're total opposites. Janine is the bookish type who is a genius when it comes to anything having to do with science or math. Claudia, on the other hand, has trouble with regular schoolwork, but she is a brilliant artist. Unfortunately, most people — including Claudia's parents — make a bigger deal about being a school genius than being an artistic genius. As a result, Claudia often feels bad about herself when she is around her sister. But since I'm also the bookish type, I was fascinated by Janine. What fascinated me the most was that she could read while she walked, just like Belle in *Beauty and the Beast*. (That movie hadn't come out yet, so Janine was the only one I knew who could walk and read at the same time.) Janine would walk to school with an open book in front of her face. I knew she was *really* reading because I'd see her turn the pages.

Claudia and Kristy liked that Janine was

reading instead of watching us. "It's just like we're walking alone," said Claudia.

"We're *very* grown-up," added Kristy.

Meanwhile, at home I was trying to teach myself to walk and read at the same time. One Saturday afternoon, my dad found me standing in the upstairs hall reading *Horton Hears a Who* by Dr. Seuss. "Mary Anne, wouldn't you be more comfortable in a chair or on the couch?"

I looked up from my book. Where was I? I'd thought I was in the Whoville town square, not the hall. "I was practicing walking and reading at the same time," I explained to my dad.

"You better stick to doing one thing at a time," he advised.

So life as a six-year-old was interesting, fun, and challenging — until the Mother's Day tea party.

One rainy April afternoon, Mrs. Frederickson announced, "Every year my first-grade class holds a special tea party for their mothers."

"I don't drink tea," Alan Gray called out.

Mrs. Frederickson yelled at Alan for not raising his hand when he had something to say. Finally, she returned to the subject of the tea. She described how we would decorate the room, what songs we would sing for our mothers, and what food we would serve. "And we'll make special invitations that you'll give to your mothers," continued Mrs. Frederickson.

I was beginning to feel *very* weird. I didn't have a mother. What would I do?

Kristy glanced my way and saw the tears forming in my eyes. Her hand shot up.

"Yes, Kristy," Mrs. Frederickson said.

"What if you don't have a mother to bring to the tea?" she asked.

"I was just getting to that," Mrs. Frederickson answered. "If you don't have a mother, or if your mother will be at work and can't take time off, you may invite another special person in your life."

Suddenly there was no need for tears. I could invite my dad to the tea. I remembered how he took a whole morning off from work for our Winter Holiday celebration at school. So I knew he'd try to take time off from work to come to the tea. Wow. A special tea party. I couldn't wait.

That night I told my dad all about the tea party. "A tea party put on by the first-graders," he said. "What a nice idea. When is it?"

"I don't remember," I replied.

"Well, find out and let me know," he said. "I'll try to arrange things at the office so I can attend." He chuckled. "I never thought of first-graders as big tea drinkers."

"You don't just drink tea," I patiently explained. "We're going to have lots of other things to drink. And to eat, too. But I can't tell you. It's a surprise."

"Excellent," he said. "I love good surprises."

As it turned out I was the one who was in for a surprise. And it wasn't a good one.

Just before lunch period the next day, Mrs. Frederickson said we should each stand beside our desk and tell the class who we were inviting to the tea party. The first three kids said they were bringing their mothers. I began to worry that I was going to be the only one who didn't have a mother to bring to the tea. But then Rita stood up and said, "I'm bringing my auntie Marie. She's my godmother." And another kid said that he was bringing his stepmother. I breathed a sigh of relief. It would be just fine for me to bring my dad to the Mother's Day tea. Especially since the girl whose turn came just before mine said she was inviting her grandmother.

My turn. I stood up and said, "I'm inviting my dad to the tea party."

Everyone in the room — except Claudia, Kristy, and Mrs. Frederickson — laughed.

"Your dad!" hooted Alan Gray. "You're inviting your dad to a *Mother's* Day tea?"

I was overwhelmed by embarrassment. How could I have been so stupid? Everyone else was bringing some kind of mother — a godmother, a stepmother, or a grandmother.

"*Class!*" Mrs. Frederickson boomed. I jumped at the sound of her voice, and sat down. "Quiet down immediately or there will be *no* Mother's Day tea party."

Through a cloud of tears I saw that Kristy was approaching Alan Gray with her fists raised. "You stupid, dummy, jerkhead," she yelled.

Alan Gray rose to his feet. His fists were raised, too.

My classmates weren't laughing at me anymore. All their attention was focused on Kristy and Alan. No one had dared fight in Mrs. Frederickson's classroom before. Now she rushed along the aisle toward Kristy and Alan, her volume rising to the decibels of a rock concert. "*Return to your seat immediately, Miss Thomas,*" she thundered.

"Why does he have to be so *dumb*?" Kristy asked, looking at the ceiling as she went to her seat.

Mrs. Frederickson was so busy restoring order to her class that she forgot *why* her students had been laughing and why Kristy was angry at Alan Gray. So Mrs. Frederickson never thought to tell me it would be perfectly fine for me to invite my dad. I was convinced that I'd make a total fool of myself and my dad if he came to our Mother's Day tea party.

CHAPTER 4

On the way home from school Kristy and Claudia talked about what a jerk Alan Gray was and how he'd ruin the tea party. "He'll probably drop a tray of cookies," said Claudia.

"And blow his nose on the napkins," added Kristy.

They made up other dumb and gross things Alan might do to ruin the party. I pretended to listen and be amused, but I was thinking about how to keep my dad from coming to the tea party.

By the time my dad arrived home that night, I had a plan. I wouldn't tell him what day we were planning to have the party. If he didn't know when it was, he wouldn't be able to come.

That night my dad didn't mention the tea party, and neither did I.

The next day in school, Mrs. Frederickson announced that our art teacher, Mrs. Packett, would help us make special invitations for the party. She showed us the art supplies she and Mrs. Packett had collected for us to use. There were little circles of paper lace, metallic sparkles, and squares of shiny paper in shades of pink, yellow, blue, and purple. We would each have a stiff sheet of white paper to work on, as well as our regular supplies: crayons, scissors, and glue. I couldn't wait to make a tea party invitation! In the next instant my heart sank. Who would I give my invitation to?

During lunch Claudia and Kristy talked about how they were going to make their invitations the most beautiful ever. "I'm going to use a lot of purple on my invitation," Claudia said. "That's my mother's favorite color."

"What's Mimi's favorite color?" I asked.

"Blue, I think," said Claudia.

"Are you inviting Mimi, too?" I asked.

"We can only bring *one* person," Kristy told me. "Mrs. Frederickson said."

That's when I got the most brilliant idea. I'd invite *Mimi* to the tea party. She was a woman, and like a grandmother to me. It was perfect. "Can I invite Mimi to the tea party?" I asked Claudia.

"What about your dad?" she countered.

"It's a *Mother's* Day tea party," I reminded her. "So I can't bring a dad."

"But didn't you invite him already?" Kristy asked.

"He forgot about it," I said. "Besides, he has to work."

"Invite Mimi then," Claudia said. "That'd be great."

"Perfect," agreed Kristy.

Kristy and Claudia seemed glad that I wasn't bringing my dad to the Mother's Day tea party. Now I knew for sure that it would have been a terrible thing to do.

I sang happy little songs in my head that afternoon as I worked on Mimi's invitation. I thought it was the prettiest thing I'd ever made.

When I walked into my house after school that day I asked my baby-sitter if I could go to Claudia's. "Just for a little while," she said. She phoned the Kishis to be sure it was okay with Mimi, then I left to deliver my invitation.

Mimi was in the kitchen cutting up vegetables for supper. "Hi," I greeted her.

"Hello, our Mary Anne," she said. "Claudia and Kristy are in Claudia's room."

"I have something for you," I said. I held out the invitation.

Mimi wiped her hands on her apron and took the invitation from me. A beautiful smile came over her face. "My, isn't this lovely!"

Please be my guest
at the
Mother's Day tea
Party

*Mimi loved this invitation
and I loved making it.*

she exclaimed. "And blue is my favorite
color."

"I know," I said.

She read the invitation out loud. Then she
said, "I would be honored to be your guest at
the Mother's Day tea party." She leaned over

and kissed me on the forehead. "Thank you for inviting me."

I ran happily up the stairs to tell Claudia and Kristy the good news. Mimi — my almost-grandmother — would be my guest.

The only person I couldn't share the good news with was my dad. For the next few days I had to be careful not to mention the tea party in front of him. It wasn't easy because during dinner my dad always asked me what I'd done in school that day. Now I had to leave out the most exciting part of the school day — preparing for the tea party. I was dying to tell him that we'd each made an illustrated book about our favorite animal that would be on display during the tea party, and that we were going to decorate the room with balloons and crepe paper. I couldn't even tell him that Kristy would be greeting people at the door, and that Claudia and I would be passing around trays of cookies.

The day before the party, Mrs. Frederickson helped us practice introducing our guests. When it was my turn I said, "I would like to introduce my neighbor and almost-grand-mother, Mimi." No one laughed. Claudia turned around and smiled at me.

Mrs. Frederickson had said that we should dress in our Sunday best for the tea party. So the next morning I put on my fancy dress with the shiny buttons. I covered it with a sweater so my dad wouldn't ask me why I was wearing my best dress to school. I looked outside. It was a beautiful spring day, not a cloud in the sky. I was allowed to wear my shiny patent leather shoes to school when the weather was good. I put them on. That morning I felt as if there were two different Mary Annes. A happy, excited Mary Anne and a sad, guilty one. The excited Mary Anne was dressing up for a special tea party. The guilty Mary Anne hadn't told her dad that she'd invited someone else, and had tricked him by not telling him the date of the party.

I felt terrible at breakfast. I couldn't wait to leave the house. Finally, Kristy rang the doorbell. It was time to go to school. I gave my dad a quick peck on the cheek. " 'Bye," I said. "See you tonight."

I was rushing to the door when my dad called after me cheerfully. "Did you forget that today's the tea party? You'll be seeing me at school this afternoon. I arranged it so that I can leave work early today."

I stopped in my tracks. "Okay," I said without turning around. " 'Bye."

I ran out of the house, past my friends, and across our lawn to the sidewalk. I wanted to get away from my house as fast as possible. I didn't want my dad to see that I was upset.

Claudia and Kristy caught up to me. "What's wrong?" asked Kristy.

"How come you're crying?" asked Claudia.

By then we'd met up with Janine, but she was reading and didn't even notice anything was wrong. Kristy, Claudia, and I walked ahead of her and talked about my problem all the way to school.

"But how did my dad even know what day the tea party was?" I asked.

We all thought about that for a minute.

"I know how," Kristy said. "The school mailed the letter they always send when there's something for parents at school. The one with directions on where to park and to remind everybody what time to be there."

"What am I going to do?" I wailed. "I can't have a dad at the tea party. And I can't invite *two* people. Mrs. Frederickson said so. I broke *two* rules about the tea party."

"Well, no one is going to laugh at you when your dad comes," Kristy growled. "I'm going to talk to Alan Gray . . ." (she raised her clenched fists) ". . . with these."

"Maybe you should tell Mrs. Frederickson what happened," suggested Claudia.

"Maybe," I said. But I was too shy to do that. Besides, maybe my dad wouldn't be able to make it at the last minute and I wouldn't have a problem after all.

Kristy gave me a tap on the arm with her fist. "Don't worry," she said. "It'll be okay."

"It will?" I said. I wasn't convinced. And judging by the worried looks on my friends' faces, I knew they weren't either.

Mrs. Frederickson was in a great mood that day. She said we all looked lovely and that she thought we even behaved better when we were dressed like ladies and gentlemen. I went through the morning with huge butterflies in my stomach. Everyone else was excited about the tea party, but I was terrified. Especially when, during penmanship, we each printed a sign in big letters with the name of our guest. "These will be your guests' place cards," Mrs. Frederickson explained. "We'll put them on their chairs."

I faced the blank piece of white cardboard. Which name should I write? "Ms. Mimi Yamamoto"? Or "Mr. Richard Spier"? Maybe I should write "Ms. Mimi Yamamoto and Mr. Richard Spier." I was sitting there pondering this question when Mrs. Frederickson, who was walking around the room to check our work, stopped at my desk. "Well, aren't you the slowpoke today, Mary Anne," she remarked.

"I don't know what to do," I admitted. Maybe, I thought, this is the time to explain that I had invited *two* guests to the party. But it was too late. Mrs. Frederickson began scolding me. "Well, you'd know what to do if you'd listened to directions instead of daydreaming."

"I'm sorry," I said.

"The instruction, Miss Spier, is to write the name of your guest. Do you understand now?"

"Yes," I answered.

After Mrs. Frederickson moved on to the next kid, I printed *Mr. Richard Spier* on the card. Then I turned it over and printed *Ms. Mimi Yamamoto* on the other side.

I was still hoping one of them wouldn't show up.

CHAPTER 5

During recess, Kristy pulled Alan Gray away from his kickball buddies. I was afraid she would get into a fight with Alan. But instead they just stood there and talked.

"What'd you say to Alan?" I asked Kristy when she walked back to Claudia and me.

"I asked him if he'd laugh if *his* mother were dead," she explained. "He said he didn't know you didn't have a mother and he won't make a joke if your dad comes to the party."

"Thanks," I said.

After lunch we went to the music room to practice the songs we would be singing at the tea. When we returned to our classroom I almost didn't recognize it. Crepe paper hung in twisted loops from the ceiling, and bunches of helium balloons floated from the corners of the bulletin boards. Our desks had been arranged in a big circle. Behind each desk, next to the student chairs, was a gray folding chair. The name tags we'd made were taped to the backs of the big chairs. I scanned the room until I read *Mimi Yamamoto*. There was only one guest chair for each student. There was no room for an extra guest.

In the middle of the circle, a round table was covered with trays of small sandwiches and cookies, stacks of paper cups and napkins, a coffeepot, a teapot, and pitchers of juice. I hoped with all my heart that my dad would have a last minute emergency at his job.

The first guests to knock on our classroom door were Claudia's mother and Mimi. I didn't want Mrs. Frederickson to think that Claudia made a mistake and invited two people, so I went straight to Mimi. I was holding Mimi's hand and showing her the book I'd written and illustrated about cats, when I heard a familiar voice say, "Good afternoon, Mrs. Frederickson."

I turned and saw my dad. He hurried to Mimi and me. "Why do you look so surprised to see me, Mary Anne?" he asked. "I told you I'd be here." He turned to Mimi. "It's nice to see you," he added.

Mimi looked from me to my dad. I stared at the floor. "It's nice to see you, too, Richard," she said.

"Mary Anne, you didn't tell me it was going

to be so fancy," my dad said. He looked around the circle of desks and chairs. I knew he was searching for his name card.

"And didn't Mary Anne make us the prettiest invitations," Mimi said. "Mine was all in blues. What color was yours?"

Fortunately, Claudia had seen the predicament I was in and she came over with her mother. Claudia took Mimi's hand. "Mimi, come see our guinea pig," she said. "Her name is Petunia."

As soon as Mimi left with Claudia, my dad asked me what was going on.

"I invited Mimi and you," I mumbled, looking at the floor. "And I'm not supposed to have two people." My eyes filled with tears. "I'm sorry."

"Come on," he said as he took my hand, "we'll straighten this out." He led me to Mrs. Frederickson. "We have a bit of a mix-up here," he told her. "Mary Anne has invited *two* people to the tea. I assume we can both stay."

I thought Mrs. Frederickson would be angry and yell at me in front of everyone. Instead she spoke softly. "Why did you invite two people?" she asked.

"I didn't think a dad could come," I explained. "So I invited Claudia's grandmother."

"Look at me, Mary Anne," Mrs. Frederickson said. I shifted my gaze from the floor to her face. She didn't look mean. "Mary Anne, it was perfectly fine for you to invite you dad to the tea. Your dad acts as both your mother *and* your father, so of course he would be the perfect person for you to bring. We'll get another chair for him and make room for it on the other side of your chair. Okay?"

"Okay," I answered. But it didn't feel okay. Especially when I had to introduce *two* people to the class and our guests. At least nobody laughed. Maybe they didn't even hear my introductions because I spoke so softly. But everyone had to have noticed that my dad was the only man in the room. I wished with all my heart that I had a mother.

My dad and I were both silent as we rode home after the tea party. Finally he said, "You're awfully quiet over there. Do you think you hurt my feelings by inviting someone else to the tea?"

I nodded.

"You didn't," he said. "I understand that you thought you should bring a woman. By the way, your teacher was very smart about something today."

"She was?"

"Yes. She knows that I have to be both a mother and a father to you."

Me with one guest too many for the Mother's Day tea party.

"I know that, too," I said.

"And I know that you feel sad sometimes that you don't have a mother," he added.

"I'm sorry," I said.

"For what?" he asked.

"That I gave my invitation to Mimi instead of you."

"I know," he said softly.

By then we'd pulled into the driveway. My dad suggested we sit in the backyard for awhile. "I'm never home at this time of day during the week," he said. "I want to enjoy it." He loosened his tie and took off his suit jacket.

I sat on my swing and he pulled the lounge chair over so he'd be near me. I knew he wanted to talk some more. "You never talk about not having a mother," he said. I could see he was sad thinking about my mother. I tried with all my might to keep from crying. I didn't want to make him any sadder. "But I know it must be difficult for you," he continued.

I dug my patent leather toe in the sand. I didn't even care that I was getting my best shoes dirty. My dad was right. It was hard not having a mother like everybody else.

"Mary Anne," my father said, "you should have told me *everything* about the problem you were having with the tea party. Then I could have helped you understand that it was okay for me to be your guest. I even would have spoken to Mrs. Frederickson about it."

"Everybody laughed when I said I was bringing my dad to a *Mother's* Day tea party," I told him.

"I bet most of those kids don't even know that you don't have a mother. If they did they wouldn't have laughed."

I remember that Kristy had to explain it to Alan Gray. "Maybe not," I agreed.

Just then Claudia came running into our yard. "Want to play?" she called out. "Mimi said it's okay. Kristy can come to my house, too."

"Since I'm home, why don't you girls play here?" my dad suggested. "Tell Mimi and Mrs. Thomas that I'll keep an eye on you." He smiled at me. "I'll even make you my famous spaghetti and meatball dinner."

"Oh, wow," said Claudia. "I'll ask Mimi."

"Can I go with Claudia?" I asked my dad.

He said yes. Claudia and I held hands and ran toward her house. "We have to tell Kristy, too," she said.

"You go ask Kristy," I suggested, "and I'll ask Mimi for you." Claudia agreed and we split up.

I entered the Kishis' kitchen. Mimi wasn't there. I went into the living room. Not there either. Was she mad at me? Was she hiding because she didn't want to talk to me?

"Well, there's our Mary Anne," I heard Mimi say. She was coming down the stairs into the living room.

"Can Claudia play at my house and stay for a spaghetti dinner?" I asked. "My dad's home and he invited her and Kristy."

"I think that's a fine idea," Mimi answered.

She sat in her rocker. "I don't think you had a very nice time at the tea party today, Mary Anne," she said.

"I'm sorry I invited two people," I replied. The tears I'd been holding back all afternoon began to flow.

Mimi motioned for me to come to her. She took a tissue from her apron pocket and patted my wet cheeks with them. "It was not the big problem for me that it was for you," she said. "So don't you worry for a minute about Mimi." She opened her arms and wrapped me in a big Mimi hug. I leaned against her and took a deep breath of her special flower smell. Then she told me that she was still honored that I invited her to the tea party and that anytime there was a function at school that my dad couldn't attend, she would be happy to fill in for him.

I wondered if all mothers and grandmothers had a special smell. Then I wondered what my mother's smell would have been like, which made me wonder if my dad had a special smell.

"I have to go home now," I told Mimi.

My father was in the kitchen. I was glad that Kristy and Claudia weren't there yet. He'd changed into his jeans and a T-shirt and was already organizing the ingredients for his spaghetti sauce.

"Where are your pals?" he asked.

"They're coming," I said.

He smiled at me. "How are you doing? Do you feel better now?"

I nodded and asked, "Daddy, can I have a hug?"

My father smiled and lifted me up into his arms. I put my arms around his neck and took in a deep breath through my nose. Yes, my dad did have a special smell. I'd have known it anywhere. It wasn't flowers, but it was spicy and fresh and it was my dad's smell. "I love you, Daddy," I whispered in his ear.

"I love you, too," my dad whispered back. "More than life itself."

Stage Fright

CHAPTER 6

I liked second
grade better than
first grade. Our
teacher, Mrs. Jeffries,
never raised her
voice and had great
ideas for helping
us learn. I did
well in all my
subjects, especially
reading and
writing, and I
was soon reading
big chapter books on
my own. I loved
going to school.

I wasn't looking forward to summer vacation half as much as Kristy and Claudia were.

"Just think," Kristy said. "In just two days we can play ball all day long."

"And draw whenever we want. It'll be *wonderful!*" Claudia shouted. She stretched out her arms and danced in big circles around her backyard, singing, "We'll be free. We'll be free."

"I'm going to practice softball every day," vowed Kristy. She threw a small rubber ball to me. I fumbled it, picked it up, and tossed it back to her. Kristy stretched to her right and managed to catch my off-the-mark throw. "I just wish I didn't have to go to that dumb old class," she grumbled.

Claudia dropped her arms and ran to Kristy. "What dumb old class?" she asked.

"At the Y," answered Kristy. "It's like a day camp, but it's only in the morning and they have classes in different stuff."

"Classes like reading and math?" I asked. I was thinking I might enjoy a day camp like that.

"They're called classes, but it's not school," Kristy said. "It's fun stuff like swimming and softball."

"That'd be okay," Claudia said enthusiastically.

But Kristy was still frowning. "My mom signed me up too late for the good classes," she said. "There wasn't any more room in swimming or tennis." She threw the ball against the garage and caught it on the bounce. "The only class that had room was ballet."

"Ballet!" exclaimed Claudia. "With tutus and everything?"

"I forgot about tutus," said Kristy with a grimace. "If it's ballet I guess we'll have to wear them."

"Oh, boy, dancing and pink tutus!" Claudia shouted happily. "Come on." She grabbed Kristy's hand. "Let's ask Mimi if I can take ballet, too."

Kristy cheered up a little. But I was feeling down. If Kristy and Claudia went to the Y every day, who would I play with?

Kristy seemed to read my mind. "Mary Anne, you can take ballet, too," she said. "If the three of us do it, maybe we'll have fun."

I tried to imagine myself doing ballet all morning, every day. I wasn't like Claudia, who loved to dance around and look in the mirror. Or like Kristy, who was athletic and enjoyed exercising. I liked to watch other people dance and do sports, but I didn't enjoy doing them myself. I wished again that school wouldn't end.

We found Mimi in the kitchen. Kristy and Claudia told her all about the ballet class. "I believe ballet class would be a good thing for you, my Claudia," Mimi said. "We'll talk about it with your parents when they come home." She smiled at me. "Are you going to ballet class, Mary Anne?"

"I don't know," I replied.

Mimi gave us each a glass of apple juice and two chocolate chip cookies. She told me, "Mary Anne, your sitter called. As soon as you finish your snack you should go home. All right?"

"Okay," I said.

We took our snacks out to the backyard and sat around the picnic table. I was feeling glum.

"Ask your dad if you can take ballet, too," Claudia urged me.

"I don't like to dance," I explained.

"If you don't do it with us you'll be alone with one of your awful baby-sitters," warned Claudia.

Kristy looked thoughtful. "Someday we can be baby-sitters," she said.

"And we'll be *good* baby-sitters," added Claudia.

"The *best*," agreed Kristy.

I did have a pretty pathetic series of sitters that year. Some of my sitters were so bad that my dad had to fire them. And every one of them was boring, boring, boring. For example,

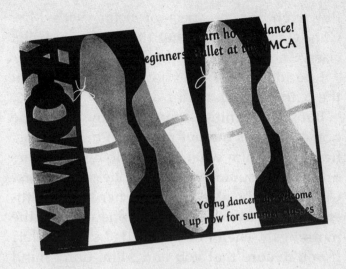

Learn how dance!
beginners ballet at the YMCA

YMCA

Young dancers welcome
n up now for summer classes

Taking ballet classes was never my idea of a fun way to spend the summer.

Mrs. Manson talked about her grandchildren all the time. They sounded as boring as she was. She also drank a lot of beer on the job. That's why my dad fired her.

Mrs. Manson was replaced by my current sitter, Mrs. Cuddy. Mrs. "Cruddy," as Kristy called her, watched TV game shows and soap operas all the time. And she was always asking me to do things for her, such as make a snack or answer the phone — which mostly rang for her. When I'd ask Mrs. Cuddy if I could play at Kristy's, she'd say, "But who will keep me company?" as if I were taking care of *her*.

61

But even the prospect of being with Mrs. Cuddy all day was better than going to ballet class.

I decided not to mention the ballet class at the Y to my dad. And I didn't.

But that evening, soon after my dad came home, Kristy's mother phoned him. She must have asked him what he was doing for sitters during the summer, because he said, "Mrs. Cuddy may be able to extend her hours. Otherwise I'll have to find someone else for the mornings." Then I heard my dad say, "Ballet? If you're sure that you and Mimi don't mind doing the carpooling back and forth, I don't see why Mary Anne couldn't do it. I would love for her to take ballet." After he hung up the phone he told me, "I'm going to sign you up for the ballet class that Kristy and Claudia are taking at the Y."

"But, Dad," I protested. "I don't know how to do ballet."

"That's the whole point of the class," he said. "To learn ballet. It's a beginners' class, so none of the kids will know ballet. I thought you'd be happy. Kristy and Claudia are going."

"I know," I said. "But I don't like to dance."

"That's why it'll be good for you," he said.

That night, when my dad kissed me good

night, he said, "I think ballet class will help you overcome some of your shyness, Mary Anne. I bet you'll love it."

I thought, if ballet can help me over my shyness, I should do it. And I did like the idea of wearing one of those pink tutus. I closed my eyes and imagined a little girl in a tutu gracefully leaping and turning across a stage. But I couldn't believe that little girl could be me.

On the last day of school Mimi picked us up. She was bringing the three of us to a special store at the mall to buy the outfits we needed for our ballet class. Claudia was still enthusiastic about dancing. And Kristy had decided that ballet class wouldn't be so bad after all. "A lot of great athletes take ballet classes," she told me. "Ballet helps athletes develop their balance and precision."

We walked across the mall to a store called Dancer's World. Kristy surveyed the window with its ballet slippers, tap shoes, and sequined leotards. "I just wish we could wear our own clothes," she said. "I play ball in jeans and a T-shirt. Why can't I dance in them?"

The *only* thing I liked about taking ballet was wearing a tutu. And there in the window, lying in a cloud of pink puff, was a tutu that looked just my size.

Claudia noticed it, too. "Wow," she breathed. "It's really pretty."

We followed Mimi into the store and were met by a young woman who asked, "May I help you?"

"We would like three tutus," Claudia piped up. "Like the one in the window."

The young woman looked at Mimi to see if our order was correct.

Instead of saying, "Yes, three tutus, please," Mimi said, "The girls are attending the beginners' ballet class at the YMCA. We were told that the staff at Dancer's World knows the regulation dance outfit. That we'd find everything we need here."

The clerk smiled at us. "You'll be in Madame Minoff's beginners' class," she said. "So you need black, cap-sleeved leotards, pink tights, and pink ballet slippers." She indicated a row of white chairs. "Sit here, girls, and I'll measure your feet."

"Don't we need tutus?" asked Claudia.

"Madame Minoff is very strict about class dress," explained the clerk. "If you wore a tutu, you'd be starting her class on the wrong foot and you'd certainly have to take the tutu off. And be sure to pull your hair back off your face for class."

Claudia was disappointed about not wearing a tutu. But she thought the pink ballet slippers were the best, and she was still excited about learning how to dance. And Kristy, who was *relieved* that we wouldn't be wearing tutus, was still happy that taking ballet would help her in sports. Especially when the clerk said she personally knew two football players and one tennis player who studied ballet.

But for me, *no* tutu meant that I had *no* reason to look forward to ballet class. All I had to look forward to was being embarrassed in front of a lot of kids, and a strict teacher named Madame Minoff.

CHAPTER 7

When I entered the kitchen Monday morning I found my father humming a cheerful, fast-paced melody. He was scrambling eggs to the tempo. "Do you know what I was humming?" he asked as he poured the eggs into the frying pan.

"No," I replied.

"It's the Dance of the Sugar Plum Fairy from the famous ballet *The Nutcracker*," he explained.

The smell of cooking eggs was making me nauseous. My stomach always gets queasy when I'm nervous. And Monday morning I was *very* nervous. It was the first day of ballet class and I didn't know what to expect or what was expected of me.

"I'm not very hungry," I told my dad.

"A good breakfast is just what you need," he said. "Best way to start the day." He put a plate of eggs and toast in front of me. "I'm so pleased you're taking this ballet class. It really helps with our summer baby-sitting situation, and you'll be doing something that's interesting and fun."

Interesting and fun? I doubted it.

An hour later I was gathered in a big studio with nineteen other little girls dressed in pink and black. A teenager named Charlene, who said she was the assistant dance instructor, organized us in a long line, one behind the other, along a *barre* in front of a mirror.

A poster under the clock announced our schedule and the class rules.

SUMMER BALLET PROGRAM-BEGINNERS

9:00-10:00	Ballet Class
10:00-10:15	Snack
10:15-11:15	Ballet Story and Video Hour
11:15-12:00	Ballet Class

RULES:
- Students must wear regulation dancewear to all classes.
- Hair must be held back from face.
- No gum chewing.
- No visiting during class.

I wanted to turn around and go home.

Three girls left the line to drop wads of gum in the basket.

Stage Fright

I was glad that the clerk at Dancer's World had told us about Madame Minoff's strict rule about hair being pulled back. My dad had pinned my braids on top of my head. Claudia, her hair in a ponytail, was standing in front of me. Kristy, her hair held back with a black headband, was behind me. Other kids who were friends had lined up near one another, too. But no one was talking above a whisper. And none of us knew what would happen next.

An elderly gentleman, with glasses perched on the tip of his nose, entered the studio and sat at the piano in a corner of the room.

Suddenly a tall, slender woman with black hair tied in a bun strode into the room. All the whispering stopped. "I am Madame Minoff," she announced. She waved a walking stick in Claudia's direction and commanded, "Two steps back, please." Madame Minoff smiled at the piano player. "Well, at least we don't have any *tutus* this summer, Mr. Riley," she commented. He answered her by smiling and hitting a few celebratory chords on the piano. A few girls giggled. I guess Claudia, Kristy, and I weren't the only ones who had thought ballet class meant wearing tutus.

After directing another girl to move two steps forward, Madame Minoff was satisfied that we were evenly spaced, and class began.

Madame Minoff explained that ballet exercises had French names, but that we would have no trouble understanding what they were since Charlene would be demonstrating the exercises for us. For the first exercises we were to hold onto the *barre* with one hand. We did *pliés*, *grand pliés*, *battements*, and *développés*. While we worked through these movements, Madame Minoff walked up and down in front of us making corrections. "Point, little one," she directed Kristy. "Stretch the toes."

I tensed whenever Madame approached me. I was terrified that she would use me to show the class how *not* to do an exercise. She'd already singled out another girl who leaned forward when she did a *grand plié*. The only correction I received from Madame Minoff during that first class was to relax the arm holding the *barre*.

At quarter to ten, Madame Minoff hit the floor with three loud taps of her stick. "To the center, young dancers," she commanded. Soon, with Charlene's help, we were spaced out in two rows with our backs to the mirrors.

For the next fifteen minutes we practiced a sequence of steps called *pas de bourrée*. It was hard for me to learn. I couldn't seem to remember when to place one foot in front of, or behind, the other. And I always seemed to finish the dance step after everyone else.

At ten o'clock the first period of our first day of ballet was over and we went out to the hallway to have a snack of apple juice and peanut butter crackers.

"Ballet's fun," said Claudia.

"It's going to make me strong," said Kristy. "All those *battements* are great for leg muscles."

I didn't say anything.

After snacks we returned to the studio to watch a video of *The Nutcracker*. Madame Minoff explained the story, which I had never heard. I loved *The Nutcracker* and even recognized the melody my father had been humming that morning. I couldn't wait to tell him. I thought, if this is ballet class, I will survive it just fine.

After ballet story and video hour we returned to our positions at the *barre* and repeated a few of the exercises we'd done during first period. "To warm up the muscles," Madame Minoff explained. Then we were back in two neat rows on the floor to practice *pas de bourrée*. "*Pas — de — bourrée*," Madame Minoff directed as she tapped her stick for each step we were to take. "One — two — three. One — two — three." I finally managed to finish the sequence when everyone else did. I was learning. I was dancing. I felt pretty good.

Two rapid hits of the stick on the floor. "Go

over to the corner of the room," Madame Min-off commanded. We did. "Now, one by one, come across the room on the diagonal. Walk three steps, starting with your left foot. Then *pas de bourrée*. And repeat. Walk — two — three. *Pas — de — bourrée*. You will do this until you reach the other side of the room. Charlene will go first to demonstrate."

One by one? I would have to dance across the floor in front of the whole class, Charlene, Mr. Riley, and Madame Minoff. I thought of asking to go to the bathroom, but that would single me out, too. My heart pounded, my face flushed, sweat gathered on my palms.

I counted the girls standing in front of me. I would be the fifth one to go, right after Clau-dia. Claudia made a mistake and Madame Minoff had her start over. But Claudia didn't seem to mind, and the second time she walked and *pas de bourrée*'d gracefully across the floor with arms extended and toes pointed just when they should be.

"Very good turnout, Claudia," Madame Minoff said. Claudia beamed as she joined the growing cluster of girls at the other end of the room. I was trembling.

Madame Minoff boomed, "Next!" She was talking to me. Mr. Riley pounded a chord to indicate I should begin. "Now," Madame Min-off barked. "First position, left foot extended, and walk. One — two — three. *Pas — de — bourrée.*" It seemed to take me a lifetime to get to the other side of the room. And my *pas de bourrées* were a mess. "That was good," Claudia whispered. But I knew it wasn't.

I'm not sure how I survived the rest of the hour. We did *pas de bourrées* across the room three more times. I longed to be home watching soap operas and game shows with Mrs. Cuddy. Anything would be better than dancing in front of other people.

On the way home, Claudia and Kristy told Mrs. Thomas all about ballet class — how they both loved it. I didn't admit that I hated and dreaded it. I was ashamed of how much it upset me to be the center of attention. I didn't even want to be the center of attention for *saying* I didn't want to be the center of attention.

As the week dragged on I could see that no one else in ballet class minded dancing in front of one another the way I did. And no one else seemed unhappy in ballet class. I didn't mind the first hour at the *barre* too much. And I thought ballet story and video hour was neat. But the hour from eleven to twelve became more and more difficult for me to endure.

I thought of asking my father if I could quit. Then I remembered how excited he was about my taking ballet classes. And how it helped him with the problem of needing baby-sitters for me in the summer. I didn't want to disappoint him by quitting. I also thought that if I stuck it out, by the end of a month of ballet classes I just might be cured of my terrible shyness.

On Thursday, Madame Minoff began stringing steps together into sequences. And each of us had to perform them for the others. On top of my embarrassment — or maybe because of it — I had trouble remembering the steps. I wasn't the worst in the class. But I came pretty close. More reason to be embarrassed.

On Friday, at the beginning of ballet story and video hour, Madame Minoff said, "We are coming to the end of our first week of ballet class, young dancers. Next week we will start learning a ballet for our recital. It will be held on the Saturday after our final day of classes. Your parents and friends will be invited, and other summer classes will be doing demonstrations and performances."

Several children clapped gleefully. Claudia whispered to me, "A recital. That'll be so much fun." She raised her hand and asked, "Madame Minoff, will we have costumes?"

"Indeed," answered Madame Minoff. "Our dance will be to the Dance of the Sugar Plum

Fairy." She smiled at Charlene. "Charlene will be the Sugar Plum Fairy." Charlene made a little curtsy and we all clapped.

Madame Minoff passed around photos of the recital from the year before, when her class also performed the dance. Everyone but me ooh-ed and aah-ed. The dancers were wearing pink tutus and sparkling sequined tiaras. The Sugar Plum Fairy wore a white silky skirt, a larger and fancier tiara, and toe shoes. My heart pounded in my chest and my hands became clammy as I looked at those photos. The Sugar Plum Fairy and her dancers were on the huge stage at the Y and the seats of the auditorium were filled with spectators.

I would have to go on a stage and dance in front of a crowd of mostly strangers! How could I dance in front of a whole auditorium of people if I was so painfully frightened dancing in front of my classmates and teacher? I had sweaty palms just *thinking* about the recital. Surely I would die. My eyes filled with tears. But no one noticed, not even Claudia or Kristy. Everyone else was too excited about being in the recital and wearing tutus.

CHAPTER 8

I woke up to the music from *The Nutcracker*. I opened my eyes. My father — a big grin across his face — was standing over me humming the melody from the Dance of the Sugar Plum Fairy. "Wake up, little Sugar Plum," he said. "I'll be in the kitchen making your breakfast. Two hours until showtime."

My heart sank. The day I'd dreaded had arrived.

I went down to the kitchen where the smell of ham and french toast greeted me. "I made you an extra special breakfast," my father said. "You have a big morning ahead of you."

I didn't have the heart to tell my dad that I didn't want breakfast. So I ate what he placed in front of me.

"Remind me to stop at the video store on the way to the Y," he said. "I need a blank tape. I'm going to videotape your part of the recital. I want to have a permanent record of your first dance performance."

"I forgot to tell you," I said. "Madame Minoff said no videotaping. Someone from the Y is going to make a videotape of us dancing. You can buy it for ten dollars." I was practically choking on the words. Not only would people be watching me onstage, but they'd be watching me over and over on their TV screens, too.

"What a good idea," my dad said. He looked at me carefully. "Your voice sounded funny just then. Are you coming down with a cold?"

I didn't tell him I was choking from fear. But I did consider saying, "Yes, I have a cold and I'd better stay home from the recital." But I stopped myself. I thought of how disappointed my dad would be if I wasn't in the recital. And how disappointed I would be in myself if I didn't overcome my fear. I took a sip of juice to clear my throat and said, "I don't think I have a cold."

"That's good," he said with a sigh of relief. "I'd hate to have you miss the recital. Do you want another piece of french toast?"

My stomach was gurgling over the two pieces I'd already eaten. "No," I managed to say. "I'm full."

My stomach gurgled again. I needed to get

away from the breakfast smells — quickly. "I better get dressed," I told my dad. And I ran up to my room.

I pulled on my pink tights and a new pink leotard. The rest of our costumes — silver-sequined tiaras and pink tutus polka-dotted with silver sequins — belonged to the Y and would be lent to us for the performance.

Madame Minoff told us to be in the studio forty-five minutes before the recital so we'd have plenty of time to put on the rest of our costumes and warm up. As we pulled into the parking spot at the Y my father said, "You're pretty quiet today, honey. Is anything wrong?"

"I'm nervous," I admitted.

He smiled. "That's normal. Even the biggest stars are nervous before a performance. They say it gives them energy to go out there and do a great job."

"Oh," I said.

We entered the Y through the main entrance. The halls were bustling with kids and adults. It seemed that everyone but me was looking forward to the recital. My father walked me to the studio.

"I'll go right to the auditorium," he said. "I want to have a good seat." He bent over and kissed me on the forehead. "I can't wait to see you onstage. I'm very proud of you."

In the studio Charlene was helping excited dancers into their tutus and tiaras. Claudia and Kristy were already wearing theirs. They ran over to me. Claudia glowed with excitement as she *pas de bourrée*'d and curtsied in front of me. Kristy seemed excited about wearing a costume and performing onstage, too. "But I still would rather play sports than be a dancer," she said.

Claudia and Kristy each took one of my hands and led me over to Charlene. It was time to put on the rest of my costume.

A few minutes later I stood at the mirror waiting to do warm-up exercises. I looked at my reflection. The tutu and tiara transformed the outside of me into a fairy princess. But the inside of me was a mass of nerves. My stomach was upset. My heart was pounding. My palms were sweaty. I was so terrified at the idea of performing onstage that I felt as if I might throw up any minute.

On the third *plié*, I let go of the *barre* and dashed out of the room.

I arrived at the toilet bowl without a second to spare. By the time I'd finished throwing up Charlene and Kristy were in the bathroom, too.

I came out of the stall feeling weak and dizzy. I leaned against the sink.

"Are you all right?" asked Charlene.

Which dancer isn't having fun?

"Mary Anne, what happened?" asked Kristy.

"I threw up," I whispered hoarsely.

"It's nerves," said Charlene. "It happened to me once, but you know what?"

"What?" I asked.

"I still went onstage and danced great. How do you feel now?"

"Okay," I replied, even though I didn't.

"Well, let's go back to the studio. You can sit out the rest of the warm-up. I bet you'll feel just fine when you're on that stage."

I wondered what would happen if I had to throw up on the stage in the middle of the Dance of the Sugar Plum Fairy. At the thought of that, I dashed back into the stall and threw up a little bit more.

When I came out, Kristy wasn't there. I figured she'd returned to the studio so she wouldn't miss too much of the warm-up. But when I went back to the studio myself, she wasn't in the lineup of tutu'd dancers doing *grand battements*.

Madame Minoff glanced my way. I gave her a weak smile and sat in the corner. She smiled back her approval.

A minute later Kristy entered the studio, followed by my father. He motioned me to come out into the hall with him. So I did.

He took my hand and squatted so he'd be

my height. "Kristy tells me you were sick, honey," he said. "What's going on?"

"I'm just nervous," I answered. "It happened to Charlene once."

"I told you that performers are often nervous before a performance," he said. "They're nervous because they're excited. Is that why you're nervous, because you're excited about being in a recital?"

I shook my head. "I'm nervous because I don't want to be in the recital. I don't like to dance in front of people, even my friends. It makes me feel too scared."

He looked upset by that idea, too. "I didn't know that."

"But I can do it, Dad," I said. "I'll be in the recital."

"If you don't want to, maybe you shouldn't," my father said. "Why should you put yourself through this?"

"I have to. It's part of ballet class. Kristy and Claudia are doing it."

"That doesn't mean you have to be in the recital."

"You want me to be in it. You said so yourself. It would make you sad if I wasn't in the recital."

"Whoa," my father said. "Hold on, there. How can I be happy about something that makes you *un*happy? I'd never want my little girl to do something that makes her so frightened she becomes sick over it. You don't have to be in the recital, Mary Anne. What do you want for yourself? Right now?"

Tears streamed down my face. I couldn't stop them. "I don't want to be in the recital, Dad," I sobbed. "I just don't."

He put his arms around me and I hugged him. "Then you shouldn't be in it, honey. I'll tell your teacher and we'll go home. Okay?"

I pulled off my tiara and handed it to him. Then I stepped out of the tutu and gave him that. "Give these to the teacher," I said. "I'll wait here for you. And tell Kristy and Claudia that I'm okay."

A few minutes later Dad and I were in the car driving home.

"Mary Anne," my father said, "I want you to make me a promise."

"What?" I asked.

"I want you to promise me that the next time you're unhappy about something you'll tell me about it. Will you promise me that?"

"I promise," I said.

My dad and I exchanged a smile. I felt so lucky to have such a wonderful father.

"Now, how's that stomach of yours doing?" he asked.

I swallowed and realized that my stomach was fine. "I feel okay," I said.

"Good," he said. "I thought maybe we'd go to the mall and buy ourselves a new barbecue grill. And then do a big grocery shopping. Maybe we could have a barbecue tonight and invite the Thomases and the Kishis. Would you like that?"

"That'd be fun," I said. "But can we go home first so I can put on my regular clothes?"

"Absolutely," he said. "I wouldn't have it any other way."

"And if it's okay, I don't want to take ballet next summer," I said. "Neither does Kristy."

"No more ballet classes," he promised.

I suddenly realized that I couldn't wait to see my friends and hear all about the recital. I wondered when they would have the video-tape to show me. I'd love to see the tape now that I wasn't in it.

I started humming the Dance of the Sugar Plum Fairy. Dad joined in. We were both happy.

E Is for Eyeglasses

CHAPTER 9

By the time I
entered fourth
grade I was a
little more self-
confident. So I
wasn't too upset
when I found out
that I was assig-
ned to a different
fourth-grade class
than Claudia and
Kristy.

"It's the first year we aren't all in the same room," complained Kristy. We were on the way to school for the first day of fourth grade. From the postcards we'd received the week before we knew that Kristy and Claudia were assigned to Class 4A with Mr. Adams and that I would be in Class 4B with Ms. Elison.

"They can't split us up," Claudia declared. "You have to be in our class, Mary Anne."

"Your dad should go to school and say he wants you in Mr. Adams' class," said Kristy.

"I don't think my dad would do that," I said. Actually, I didn't want to be taken out of Ms. Elison's class. I'd watched her with her classes at school assemblies and in the schoolyard. And once she'd visited our class to tell us about a city-wide poetry contest. To me Ms. Elison was the perfect teacher. She was smart, pretty, self-confident, and cheerful. I wasn't going to give up being in Ms. Elison's class for anything.

"Welcome to fourth grade," Ms. Elison said when I walked into her beautifully decorated classroom on the first day of school. I looked around. One bulletin board told me we'd be studying American history and from another I learned that we'd be studying poetry. I couldn't wait to learn American history and poetry from Ms. Elison.

. "Find the desk with your name card on it and take your place, please," Ms. Elison directed.

I found the desk labeled "Mary Anne Spier" and sat down. I checked out my fourth-grade classmates. I counted fifteen kids I'd been in classes with before, including Alan Gray. And I recognized all but one of the other ten kids. The one girl who was totally new to me — and to the school — was sitting at the desk next to mine. I sneaked a look at the name card on her desk and read, "April Livingston." I'd never met a girl named April before. I wondered if I'd ever met anyone named after a month. I reviewed the months of the year in my head. Nope. I hadn't even met a "May" or a "June."

April had curly brown hair pulled back in a loose ponytail with a red ribbon. She wore jeans and red high-top sneakers. Her light blue sweatshirt announced, "I swam with dolphins." I was already fascinated by April Livingston.

After the principal welcomed us to a new school year over the public address system, Ms. Elison explained our first activity as a class. She would assign us each a partner. The partners were to interview one another and take notes. We would then have fifteen minutes to organize our notes into a paragraph of introduction of the person we interviewed. Then the pairs would go to the front of the room and introduce one another to the class.

Ms. Elison called out the names of the pairs. I hoped with all my heart that Alan Gray would *not* be my partner. "Mary Anne Spier and April Livingston," Ms. Elison announced. I looked in April's direction. She smiled and gave me a thumbs-up sign. I smiled back.

Giving a speech in front of the room is not a good way for a shy person like me to start off a new school year. But I tried not to think of the standing-in-front-of-the-room part of the assignment. Instead I concentrated on how interesting it would be to find out all about the new girl.

Before we broke up into pairs, the whole class worked on a list of questions we might ask each other. We copied the questions into our notebooks as Ms. Elison wrote them on the board. Finally, April and I pushed our desks together and we were ready to interview one another.

"You ask me questions first," suggested April.

"Okay," I agreed. I opened my notebook and began.

April was fun to interview and I liked everything I learned about her. Her hobbies were biking, swimming, drawing cartoons, and reading. She wanted to be a comedian and an actor when she grew up. And she thought Stoneybrook was a fun town. She had an older sister and a younger sister and got along fine with both of them. The most fun she ever had was swimming with the dolphins in Florida. The nicest thing that ever happened to her was getting a puppy on her sixth birthday, a golden retriever named Alex. The saddest thing that ever happened to her was that her grandmother had died during the past summer.

"Now I'll interview you," said April. She reached into her desk and took out a silver glasses case. She opened the case and put on a pair of red-rimmed glasses. April's fun-filled, smiling face brightened up even more with the sparkle of the red frames.

"I like your glasses," I said.

"I just got them," she told me. "I'm always forgetting to put them on." She looked around the room and joked, "Ah, everything is clear now." She smiled at me. "You're even prettier than I thought." She laughed. "And you blush."

"I'm shy," I explained. "I hope I introduce you to the class okay."

"Don't worry," she said. "You can go first so you can get it over with. Anything you forget, I'll say. No problem."

And it wasn't a problem. I wanted to tell everyone all about April. And I wasn't half as nervous as I usually am talking in front of a class. Instead of looking at me, the class was watching April do gestures for everything I said about her. For example, when I said she had two sisters, she held up two fingers. And when I said she liked to read she pretended she was reading a book. And when I said the part about the dolphins she imitated swimming *and* being a dolphin.

When I'd finished my introduction of April, she said, "Mary Anne, don't forget to say I'm outgoing and friendly." Everyone laughed. They were enjoying our introductions.

I blushed while April introduced me. But I liked when she said, "Mary Anne is quiet, but loads of fun to be with. In her own way, she's outgoing and friendly, too."

"Very nice, girls," Ms. Elison said. "You both did that splendidly."

During math class it started to rain, so we had recess in our room. I asked April, "Can I try on your glasses?"

"Sure," she said.

I put them on. The frames felt good on my face. I loved wearing glasses. "They look great on you," said April. I took them off and put them carefully back in the case. A whole bunch of girls came over to April's desk. They all wanted to talk to her.

"I have to sharpen my pencil," I told April. "I'll be right back." I made sure to take the glasses with me to the pencil sharpener, which was right next to a window. I checked to see that none of the kids was looking at me. No one was. I put the glasses on again and took a quick peek at my reflection in the window. But the image was blurred because of April's prescription, so I couldn't see just how great I looked in glasses.

April wore her glasses for English class. Every time I looked at her, which was often, I admired how neat she looked. I noticed that Ms. Elison wore glasses too. Hers were rimmed in a dull silver and looked perfect with her black hair. Ms. Elison only used her glasses for reading, so she was always putting them on and taking them off. I loved how she dangled them from her hand when she spoke to us, then put them on her face to read a poem. I wished I wore glasses.

That afternoon on the way home I compared notes with Kristy and Claudia about the first day of school. I didn't tell them about April. Kristy was my very best friend and I didn't want her to be jealous.

"Are you coming over to my house?" asked

Kristy when we were nearly home.

"In a little while," I said. "First I've got to do something."

"What?" asked Kristy.

"I have to tell Patricia I'm home."

Patricia Pennybrook, my current baby-sitter, was a huge improvement over some of my other sitters. She started sitting for me two weeks before school started. Patricia said sitting for me was the perfect job because I was so well behaved and didn't need a lot of attention, which meant she had lots of time to do her homework for college. She almost always let me go to Kristy's or Claudia's instead of staying at home with her.

I found Patricia sitting at the kitchen table, studying. "Want a snack?" she asked.

"No," I answered as I flew past her. "Gotta do something in my room. Then I'm going over to Kristy's."

"Okay," she agreed without looking up from her book.

I opened the bottom drawer of my bureau and went through my things until I found what I was looking for. My purple-framed sunglasses. I put them on and studied my image in the mirror. I liked how I looked in the sunglasses. But since I couldn't see my eyes through the dark lenses, it wasn't the same as seeing myself in *real* glasses.

I thought I'd look cute in glasses.

My school photo from last year was stuck in my mirror next to Claudia's and Kristy's. I took my picture to my desk, and with a red Magic Marker drew glasses around the eyes. Wow! I looked great in glasses.

The next day, during recess, I asked April if I could borrow her glasses again. She said yes. I carefully put her glasses case in my jacket pocket. We all streamed out to the schoolyard. I stuck close to April. So did a lot of other girls. It was already clear that April would be the most popular girl in our class. One of the neat things about April was that she was nice to everyone, not just a few of the more popular girls.

A group of us, including Kristy and Claudia, were standing around deciding what game to play, when I put on April's glasses. One girl said, "I didn't know you wore glasses, Mary Anne."

"I don't," I said. "These are April's."

"They look great on you," said Claudia. "Can I try them on?"

We spent the rest of recess trying on April's glasses. On the way back to our classroom I made sure to walk next to April. "I wish I wore glasses," I told her.

"They can be a pain sometimes," she said. "I'm always forgetting where I put them."

"But they look really neat on you."

April flashed her great smile at me. "Thanks," she said.

That weekend my father and I went on a shopping trip to the discount pharmacy. While my dad was picking out the things we needed, I discovered a rack of reading glasses. I tried on a pair. I thought they looked pretty good, but it was hard to tell.

"Can I help you?" asked a clerk.

"No, thank you," I replied. "I'm just looking."

"Just *looking?*" he said. He laughed. "Well, let me know if I can help you, young lady. By the way, that pair looks nice on you."

"Thanks," I said.

I took off the glasses and looked at my now clear reflection in the display's oval mirror. I wasn't blushing. I checked my hands. They weren't clammy. I'd had that entire conversation with the clerk without having a shy attack. I thought, wearing glasses could change my life.

Monday morning Ms. Elison announced, "This week our school is conducting vision screening tests for all students. You will be tested on Wednesday morning."

A vision test! I couldn't believe my good luck. Maybe they'd discover I needed glasses. The test was on Wednesday. By Friday I might have my own pair of glasses. But what if I passed the test? What if I didn't need them? Suddenly I had an idea of how to make sure that I would soon be wearing glasses.

CHAPTER 10

If I wanted eyeglasses — which I did — I would have to fail the vision test on purpose. But to fail I needed to know in advance what the test was like.

When our class was on the way to phys ed on Tuesday, I noticed a few third-graders lined up outside the nurse's office. I figured they were waiting for their vision test.

During lunch hour the third-graders were out in the schoolyard with us. Jennifer Searles, a girl I knew from our block, was off by herself jumping rope. I went over to her.

"Did you do that vision test thing yet?" I asked.

"Yeah," she answered. "I read every line perfectly."

"What's the test like?" I asked.

"You have to read these letters. They don't spell anything. They get smaller and smaller until they're real teeny. But I could see those, too."

"Is it one of those charts with the big E on top?" I asked.

"Yeah," Jennifer said.

I'd taken that vision test at my pediatrician's office. It was easy and I'd passed it without any trouble. So I probably would pass this test, too. Now that I knew what the test was like, I needed a plan to fail it.

After school I told Kristy and Claudia that I had to do some homework before I could play outside. I didn't tell them that my "homework" was to figure out how to *fail* a test.

I sat at my desk. First, I decided that I should read the first few lines of the vision test correctly. Otherwise the tester might guess I was trying to fail it. Then on the third or fourth line I'd start making mistakes.

Now, how should I make the mistakes? It would look fishy if my mistakes were huge errors like saying a T was an O. I printed out the letters of the alphabet in a row. Then I squinted my eyes until the letters weren't clear. I saw that with poor vision an M could look like an N, and that an E could be mistaken for an F. I squinted my way through the whole alphabet deciding what to say for the different letters.

By the time I went over to Claudia's to play, I was confident that I could fail the vision test with flying colors. I couldn't wait for tomorrow to come.

The next morning, right after announcements, Ms. Elison told us that we were taking our vision test first thing. She explained that only three of us would be out of the room at a time — two waiting outside the nurse's office and one taking the test. "As soon as one of you comes back from the test the next person will leave," she said. "The first three in the first row may leave now. The rest of you will start the math exercise that is written on the front board."

I was the third person in the first row, so I followed Jack Luke and Maria Gonzalez out of the room.

Maria and I waited outside the nurse's office while Jack took the test. When he came out, I asked him if it was one of the charts with the E at the top. "Uh-huh," he said. "It's easy."

A few minutes later Maria had finished the test. "Your turn," she said to me. "I think I passed. It was easy." I thought, I hope it's easy to fail, too.

Our school nurse, Mrs. Randolph, was testing us. She told me to sit in the chair in the middle of the room facing the eye chart. She

```
┌─────────────────────────┐
│                         │
│           E             │
│                         │
│      K Q M E R T Y       │
│                         │
│     R T M U L K X C      │
│                         │
│       M O F B H          │
│                         │
│      E A D G J S Z P S   │
│                         │
│     I W L C N F T A V Q R │
│                         │
└─────────────────────────┘
```

The only test I tried to fail.

pointed to the E at the top of the chart and asked, "Which way does the open side of the E face — toward the door or toward the bookshelves?"

"Toward the door," I answered.

"Good. Now read the letters on the next line."

"K, Q, M, E, R, T, Y," I said confidently.

"Very good, Mary Anne," Mrs. Randolph said. She tapped the chart with a wooden pointer. "Now, the next line."

I quickly looked down the chart and counted that there were four more lines. I decided to get all the letters on this line right, but that I would take longer to read them.

"R . . . T, M, W . . . no that's a U . . . L, K, X, C," I said.

"Didn't your teacher tell you that you should wear your glasses for the test?" Mrs. Randolph asked.

"But I don't wear glasses, Mrs. Randolph," I told her.

"Oh," she said. She looked puzzled and concerned. "Well, let's do the next line. Take your time."

I took a deep breath. Even though I could read the line clearly, I said the M was N and that the O was a Q. I read the next letter correctly, but followed it by two more mistakes.

"All right, Mary Anne," Mrs. Randolph said. "You've finished the test." She was frowning and writing something on my chart.

"Don't you want me to read the next line?" I asked. I already knew that the first letter was E, which meant I would say it was a B.

"No, that's fine, dear." She gave me a sympathetic smile.

I knew I had failed the test beautifully. Soon I would have my own glasses. I couldn't wait. I wondered if the school would let me pick out my own frames. If they did I couldn't decide if I wanted red frames or horn rimmed ones like the pair I noticed Claudia's mother wore. Or maybe I wanted silver ones like Ms. Elison.

At the end of the school day, Ms. Elison called Jeanette Thompson and me to her desk. I wondered if I'd be wearing my new glasses home.

"Girls," said Ms. Elison, "the vision test you took this morning indicates that you have vision problems. Did you notice that you had difficulty reading the eye chart?"

I smiled and nodded.

"Uh-huh," said Jeannette. She didn't look very happy about it.

"Can we pick out the frames for our glasses?" I asked Ms. Elison.

"That's really up to your parents," she said. "First you need to see your family eye doctor for further testing. Bring these notes to your parents." She handed each of us a note.

Further testing? Family eye doctor? I thought the school would give me glasses. But instead I had to go to a special eye doctor. What kind of test would the eye doctor give me? Would that doctor figure out that I had failed the school vision test on purpose? Would the eye doctor tell my father? I was confused and worried. It was a lot harder to get a pair of glasses than I thought it would be.

CHAPTER 11

That night I gave my father the note from school. He seemed worried and a little upset by it. He asked me if I had trouble reading the board in school. I couldn't lie to my father. "I can read the board okay," I told him. Then he asked me to read different-sized print in the newspaper. I could read them all.

"It doesn't seem to me as if you have a serious vision problem," he told me. "But we better have it checked out as soon as possible."

The next evening my father told me I had an appointment with a Dr. Crews on Saturday morning. There was one more day of school before Saturday. I'd ask April what it was like to go to an eye doctor.

April explained that I'd have to read an eye chart. She also described a machine that was like glasses and how the doctor would keep changing lenses and asking her to tell him when rows of letters were clear and when they were fuzzy.

"The test takes a long time," April said. "But it doesn't hurt or anything."

I realized there was no way I could prepare to fail this test. I would have to figure it out as I went along. Maybe I'd say the fuzzy images were clear and the clear ones were fuzzy. But I wasn't sure that would work. Since Dr. Crews was an expert on vision, I figured he'd know if someone was making a mistake on purpose.

On the way home from school, Claudia and Kristy were all excited that it was the weekend. "My mom said she'd take us to Brenner Field to play tomorrow morning," said Kristy. "Let's invite April."

"I have to go the the doctor's tomorrow," I told them.

"How come?" asked Claudia. "Are you sick?"

"I have to go to an eye doctor," I explained. "I might need glasses."

"Oh," said Claudia.

"Too bad," Kristy sympathized.

"But you did look nice in April's glasses," Claudia said.

"Lots of people have to wear them," added Kristy.

I could tell they were trying to make it seem as if it were okay that I needed glasses, but they really didn't think so. Didn't they think it would be fun to wear glasses?

Saturday morning, on the way to the eye doctor, my father asked me to read him the signs on shops we passed. "Your distance vision seems fine," he said. He patted me on the leg. "Don't worry, honey, whatever the problem is with your vision, glasses will take care of it. I think you'll look very nice in glasses. A real intellectual."

"Thanks, Dad," I said. I wasn't sure what I was thanking him for. I was too nervous to carry on an intelligent conversation. What if I couldn't fail the vision test? Would the doctor know that I had cheated in order to fail it in school? Would he tell my father and report me to the school authorities?

There was a man, another child and his mother, and a receptionist in the doctor's waiting room. Near the receptionist's desk I noticed a rack of glasses frames. I went over to look at them.

"The ones on the two bottom rows are your size," the receptionist said. "There aren't any lenses in them. You're welcome to try them on."

I would finally be able to see how I looked in real glasses! I tried on the red frames first.

I looked in the mirror expecting to be pleased by what I saw. But I wasn't. My whole face was covered with two red circles. I didn't look great in glasses after all. In fact, I thought I looked terrible. I tried on the horn-rimmed glasses. I looked like a racoon!

I didn't see any frames that were dull silver like Ms. Elison's. Suddenly, I didn't want glasses. First of all, I didn't think I looked good in them. And secondly, they didn't make me feel less shy after all. I was totally embarrassed standing there trying them on. In fact they made me feel more shy.

"Why don't you try on that pink pair?" suggested the receptionist. "They're second from the right in the first row."

"No, thanks," I mumbled. I made a beeline for the chair next to my dad's

What was I going to do? I didn't want glasses, but I had failed the vision test at school and now I was at the eye doctor's. I decided that I would do the best I could on the test. I would pass it on purpose and I wouldn't need glasses. My only problem then was that the doctor might tell my father and my school that I must have failed the other test on purpose. Still, I made up my mind to pass the doctor's vision test. I didn't want glasses. Period. The end. I shuddered remembering how awful I looked in them.

"Did you like any of the frames?" my father asked.

"Nope," I answered. I swung my feet back and forth and studied my lap. "They all look awful."

"Cheer up," he said. "Maybe you won't need glasses."

I looked up at him and grinned. My father wouldn't be upset that he took me all the way to the doctor to learn that I *didn't* need glasses.

"I bet I don't need them, either," I told him.

"Mary Anne Spier," the nurse announced. "This way, please."

"I'll wait here," my dad said.

I followed the receptionist down the hall and into the examining room.

"I'm Dr. Crews," said the young man who greeted me. He pointed to a chair that reminded me of the haircutting chairs in beauty parlors. "Sit here, Mary Anne." The room was filled with all kinds of equipment, including the machine that April had described.

The first part of the test was similar to the vision chart at school. Rows of letters, like those on the chart, were projected on the wall one line at a time. I did great for a whole bunch of lines. Then there was a row of letters that I couldn't read. But they were such tiny letters, I figured no one else could have read them either.

For the next part of the test, Dr. Crews pulled a machine down in front of my eyes and had me look through it. Then he put in lenses and asked me to look at the wall again. He projected on the wall two identical rows of letters that he called "one" and "two" and asked me which was clearer. This part of the test went on for a long time. I couldn't wait for the eye test to be over and for Dr. Crews to tell my father that I didn't need glasses. Maybe I'd ask my dad to bring me to the park so I could meet up with my friends and tell them the good news.

"Well, Mary Anne," Dr. Crews said. "We're almost finished here." He swung the machine away from my eyes. "Your school nurse was correct in recognizing that you need glasses, but you'll only need them for reading." He put a pair of heavy glasses on my face and handed me a page with paragraphs in different-sized print. "Read the third paragraph for me," he said. I did. Then he took the glasses off. "*Now* read it." Without the glasses the words were all fuzzy and I had to strain to read it. Dr. Crews was right. I needed glasses. He was writing something on a prescription pad. "Let's go explain everything to your father," Dr. Crews said.

I couldn't believe it. Glasses? Me? I thought I had great vision! I had only wanted glasses for the fun of it and because I thought I'd look good in glasses. But now I didn't want to have anything to do with *glasses*.

Still, half an hour later I was at Washington Mall going into a store called Out of Sight Eyewear.

"They can have your lenses made up in an hour," my dad explained. "But first you have to pick out frames."

Out of Sight Eyewear had hundreds of frames. I didn't know where to begin. "Let's ask for help," my dad suggested.

A young woman handed me frame after frame. I was so upset by the idea of having to wear glasses that it was hard to pick out frames. As far as I was concerned every pair I tried on looked terrible on me. Finally, I narrowed my choice down to three frames. I tried each of them on for my dad. "You pick," I told him.

"The pair with the brown rims," he said. "I like the way they match your hair."

Dad and I walked around the mall and ate pizza while my glasses were being made up. I was pretty depressed. I'd even missed playing with my friends at the park. They'd have left by now. But an hour later I owned a pair of horn-rimmed glasses in a bright blue case.

"I'm glad we caught your vision problem early on," my dad said as we drove onto Bradford Court. "It would be a shame to have you straining your eyes to read. That could create an even worse problem."

"Uh-huh," I said. I opened the car door and stepped out. It was a beautiful fall afternoon, but I wasn't happy. I hated that I had to wear glasses.

Kristy's three-year-old brother, David Michael, ran toward me. "Mary Anne, Mary Anne, I want to see your glasses."

"How do you know I have glasses?" I asked.

"Kristy said. Please, I want to see your glasses."

I opened my blue case and showed David Michael the glasses. "Put them on," he ordered.

I did. Even in front of a three-year-old kid I felt myself blush. David Michael grinned at me and said, "You look like a grown-up."

"Thanks," I said. "See you later."

I took my glasses off and turned to go into the house. David Michael pulled on my jacket. "You have to go show Kristy," David Michael told me. "Kristy said."

After telling my dad where I was going, I went over to the Thomases' and up to Kristy's room. Claudia, Kristy, and April were sitting on the floor with their backs to me. I could see they were cutting out something, but I couldn't tell what it was. Kristy wasn't the type to play with paper dolls. And I didn't think April was either. I decided that Claudia had gotten them involved in an art project.

"Hi," I greeted them. "I'm back."

The three of them turned around and looked up at me through huge, handmade cardboard glasses frames. "Hi!" they shouted.

"We made a pair for you," Claudia said. "Put them on." She handed me a pair of bright red cardboard frames decorated with sequins and tiny stars.

We stood at Kristy's bureau mirror and looked at ourselves. We totally cracked up.

When we finally stopped laughing, Claudia asked, "Did you need glasses, Mary Anne?"

I nodded. "For reading."

"Mine are for distance," said April. "Let's see yours."

I opened the case and showed them.

"Put them on," they ordered in unison.

I took off the goofy glasses and put on my real glasses.

"They look neat on you," said Claudia.

"The brown frames match your hair," added April.

"You look so smart in glasses," said Kristy. "People can tell you like to read and everything."

"Just like Ms. Elison," April remarked.

I can tell when my friends are telling the

At least my new glasses
didn't look like these!

truth and when they're saying something just to make a person feel better. They were telling the truth about my glasses.

"Thanks," I said.

I took my glasses off, put them carefully back in their case, and snapped the case closed. Maybe wearing glasses wouldn't be so bad after all.

Exploring My Secret Past

CHAPTER 12

Up until this year
I know very little
about my mother
and I thought that
my father was my
only living relative.
Recently I learned
things about my
mother and my
past that have
changed my life
forever.

M_y dad and I rarely talked about my mother. I knew that was because it made him sad. But I was sad, too — sad that I hardly knew anything about my own mother. I wasn't even sure what she looked like. There weren't any pictures of her around the house. I vaguely remembered seeing a photo album of their wedding, but it was so long ago that I couldn't even remember when or how I happened to see it.

When Stoneybrook was preparing for Heritage Day I became even more curious about my mother. My friends and the kids we babysit for were looking into their own family histories. Mine was one big blank.

Then I had the idea to look through boxes in our attic to see if my father had saved anything that would tell me about my family history. I knew it was a sneaky thing to do, but I felt it was the only way I could learn about my own roots. So one afternoon, when I was alone in the house, I checked out the attic. Most of the boxes up there belong to Sharon and Dawn, but finally I spotted an old cardboard box that was labeled "Miscellaneous" in my father's neat handwriting.

The first thing I found in the box was a photo album. I opened it. The first few pages were photos of my parents' wedding. Seeing my mother's picture took my breath away. Even though she's an adult in those pictures I could see that I looked like her. Soon I came to a few photos of my parents with me as an infant.

Next came two pages of pictures of baby-me with another couple. I looked carefully at their faces, but I didn't recognize them. In one photo, I'm on the shoulder of the man who's standing between two high rows of corn. In another, the woman and I are petting a baby goat. In still another, I'm sitting on a porch step between the man and woman. Who were those people? Where did they live? And what was I doing with them?

Next came two pages of pictures of a birthday party. I was in all the pictures. I was sure it was me because I had on my "Mary Anne" necklace. The birthday cake had a single big candle. These were pictures taken at a party celebrating my first birthday! There were about a dozen adults and children whom I didn't recognize, including the mystery couple. But my father wasn't in any of those photos. Why not? There were two more pages of me in the album. Sometimes I'm alone and sometimes I'm with the man and woman. Who were they?

Clues to a past
I don't
remember.

"Mary Anne!" a voice shouted. I was startled out of the past. It was my father. He and Sharon were home!

I flushed with nervousness and shame. I didn't want them to know that I was snooping in the attic. I quickly shut the box, ran out of the attic, and yelled down the stairs. "I'm in my room. I went to bed early." I did go to bed after that. But I didn't sleep. I was more confused than ever about my past.

I didn't return to the attic the next day or the day after that. For the next week, as I helped my baby-sitting charges explore their own family histories, I tried to shove aside the questions I had about mine. But I couldn't forget the photos I'd seen, and at odd moments I would remember the box in the attic and wonder what other secrets it held about my past.

I was also thinking a lot about my mother. I realized that I didn't even know where her grave was in the cemetery. Mimi had died recently. I thought about how the Kishis often visited her gravesite. I wanted to visit my own mother's grave.

One afternoon I biked to the cemetery to look for it. I searched up and down rows and rows of grave markers, but I couldn't find a gravestone for Alma Baker Spier. I ended up crying over Mimi's grave. I realize now that losing Mimi was one of the reasons that I had been thinking about my own mother so much lately. In a lot of ways, Mimi had replaced the mother I never knew. Now Mimi was gone, too, and one loss was reminding me of the other.

When I left the cemetery I headed directly home to revisit the box in the attic. I wanted to learn whatever I could about my past, even if it was confusing and painful. And believe me, what I learned in the attic that afternoon *was* confusing and painful.

First, I looked at the pictures again. But they didn't tell me any more than they had before. So I opened another box which was marked "Correspondence." I took out a bundle of letters that lay on top and were all addressed to my father. I sat back on my heels and began to read them.

I figured out from those letters that the man and woman were Verna and Bill Baker. They were my mother's parents, which made them my grandparents! I learned that after my mother's funeral, my father had asked them to take care of me. They'd agreed and taken me with them to their farm in Iowa. Verna and Bill had raised me instead of my own father! I was shocked by this news. Why hadn't my father told me that I didn't live with him when I was little? Why had he given me away in the first place? How could he?

I read a couple of letters from Verna telling my father little details about my baby life. In one letter she went on for a whole page about how I'd taken my first step before my first birthday. I guess she didn't realize that he didn't care. After all, he hadn't even bothered to go to my first birthday party. He didn't want me!

Realizing that my father had given me away was so upsetting that I ran out of the attic without going through the rest of the box. It was difficult to face my father at dinner, but I managed to pretend nothing was wrong. I couldn't sleep that night thinking about how my father had given me away. I was also perplexed. Why had he taken me back? Had my grandparents died and he had no choice? Was the only reason that I lived with my father because he couldn't find anyone else to take care of me?

Around two in the morning I returned to the attic to find the answers to these questions. What I learned made me feel a little better — at least temporarily. The rest of the letters from Verna to my father told me that when I was about eighteen months old my father told my grandparents he was ready to take care of me himself. My grandparents were afraid my father couldn't handle raising a child on his own. But my father insisted that I belonged with him and even hired a lawyer to explain it to my grandparents. (That's the part that made me feel better.) My grandparents were unhappy about giving me up, but finally they agreed and I moved back to Bradford Court. I put the letters back in the box.

The next afternoon I accidentally overheard a phone conversation between Verna Baker — my grandmother — and my father. Had my father been in touch with her all these years? I wondered. And if so, why hadn't he told me about my grandparents and why hadn't I ever seen them the way other kids see their grandparents?

By listening in on their phone call, I learned that my grandmother and father hadn't spoken to one another for many years. My grandmother was calling now to tell my dad that my grandfather had died. She said that she wished my grandfather had seen me before he died and that she wanted me to visit her now. My father objected and said that it wouldn't be good for me. Verna sounded angry and scolded my dad.

Quietly I hung up the phone. I was afraid they'd hear me crying. I couldn't believe it. My grandmother was alive. The one who hadn't wanted to give me up eleven and a half years ago. And now she wanted me back. But she didn't sound like a nice grandmother. She sounded mean.

It took a day or two for me to build up the courage to confront my father about what I had learned from the box in the attic and from the phone conversation he'd had with my grandmother. I needed his reassurance that he really did want me to live with him. And I had to tell him my fear that my grandmother had some legal claim to me. Would I have to go live with her?

My father was pretty surprised about my discoveries. But he also seemed relieved to have everything about my past out in the open. He explained that I wouldn't have to live with my grandmother — whether she wanted it or not. But as far as he could tell, all she wanted was for me to spend a few weeks with her. She didn't want to die without knowing her only grandchild. I asked him why, if she was so anxious to see me, they hadn't kept in touch with us all those years.

My father said that at first my grandparents were very angry at him for taking me away. "And Iowa is clear across the country," he added. "They couldn't have seen you without seeing me. If they lived nearby it might have been different."

"But lots of kids only see their grandparents once a year," I protested.

My father explained that losing me was a big loss for Verna and Bill. "And it came on top of losing their own daughter," he said. "I guess they felt visiting you only once a year or so just would have made them sadder. We could all see you were going to look like your mother."

I learned then that I reminded my father of my mother. But he said he liked that, and he thought my grandmother would, too. We hugged and cried.

After that conversation I thought about my grandmother a lot. I loved the idea that I had a grandmother — a grandmother who had loved and cared for me when I was an infant. A grandmother who — even though she wanted to raise me herself — agreed to let me return to my own father. I wondered if I would love her as much as I loved Mimi. Of course I would, I thought. She's my own flesh and blood. She's my mother's mother.

I'd done a lot of snooping around to learn my family history. But there was still one letter — the most important letter — that I hadn't read. It was a letter my mother wrote to me before she died. She'd told my father to give it to me when I was sixteen. But he decided that if she had known how mature I'd be at thirteen, she would want me to have it. He called me into his study and gave it to me.

The letter is four pages long. Here's a part of it:

> I had a wonderful childhood. My parents — your grandparents — are terrific, loving people. They gave me a very happy childhood and I know that they will do whatever they can to make your childhood a happy one.
> Isn't the farm wonderful? I had so many fun-filled hours playing in the fields and tending the animals. And isn't my mother the most fabulous cook? Knowing that you have your father and my parents when I'm no longer here is a great comfort to me.

After I finished reading my mother's letter (and crying) I went to find my father. He was sitting on his couch in his study, in exactly the same position he was in when I'd left him half an hour before. I knew he'd been thinking about how my mother was speaking to me from the past through her letter. He must have remembered the day she wrote it and asked him to save it for me. I could see that he'd been crying, too.

I spoke first. "Thank you for giving me my mother's letter. You can read it if you want." He shook his head no.

I sat next to him on the couch. "I want to know all about her, Dad. But don't worry, I won't ask you a lot of questions. I know it's hard for you to talk about her."

He looked at me with sad eyes. "It's okay, honey," he said. "Ask me anything. I only want what's best for you."

"I want to visit my grandmother," I said.

A wave of hurt and panic crossed his face, but I continued anyway. "I want to be with her. Especially now that Bill . . . my grandfather . . . is dead. She's all alone in the world. Please, Dad."

He cleared his throat. "I don't know, Mary Anne. I don't know if that's such a good idea." His voice sounded far away, as if he were talking to himself. "I guess we all made the wrong decision by not keeping you in touch with your grandparents. But that was what Verna and Bill wanted. They could have written a letter or picked up the phone at any time, just as Verna did yesterday." There was fear in his eyes. "What if you go there and don't want to come back? If you wanted to live with her, I'd have to let you."

"I'm not going there to live with her, Dad," I said. "I'm just going for a visit. Don't you think my mother would want me to go?"

"Yes," he whispered, "of course she would." He was silent for a few seconds, then he said, "Maybe you could go next winter. During school vacation."

"I want to go as soon as possible," I said. "Before school starts. I can't wait to meet my grandmother."

I could see that my wanting to visit my grandmother hurt my father's feelings. But I didn't understand why. I thought my dad was being selfish. He'd had me to himself all these years. Now it was Verna's turn to spend some time with her very own granddaughter. The granddaughter she'd wanted to raise and hadn't seen in eleven years.

The next day my father bought me a round trip plane ticket to Iowa. "Verna will meet you

Issued by: **BLUE SKY AIRWAYS**				**BLUE SKY AIRWAYS**
Name of Passenger: MARY ANNE SPIER				
FROM—TO	AIRLINE	FLT.	DATE	TIMES
Stamford, CT—Des Moines, IA	Blue Sky Airways	652	FRI AUG 9	DEP 3:24 PM ARV 4:44 PM
Seat 14 B Coach Class	Non-smoking			
Des Moines, IA—Stamford, CT	Blue Sky Airways	115	MON AUG 19	DEP 9:55 AM ARV 1:15 PM
Seat 10 D Coach Class	Non-smoking			
THANK YOU FOR CHOOSING BLUE SKY AIRWAYS				

A ticket to the unknown.

at the airport," he told me. "You leave in two days. Is that soon enough?"

I gave him a big hug. "Thank you, Dad," I said.

My dad was pretty mopey over the next two days. But I was just the opposite of mopey. I was overwhelmed with excitement. I told all my friends about my grandparents and the complicated story of my childhood. They thought it was pretty wonderful that I'd discovered my long-lost grandmother. Dawn helped me pack and on Friday afternoon I was on a plane headed west toward Iowa.

As the plane flew above piles of clouds, I felt close to my mother. It was almost as if I were going to visit her. I'd see where she'd grown up. I might even stay in her bedroom. And I would learn so much about her from my grandmother. My grandmother and I talking about my mother. I couldn't wait.

CHAPTER 13

It was easy to pick out my grandmother in the crowd of people waiting for Flight 652. She looked just the way she did in the photos I'd seen. My grandmother recognized me, too. I ran over to her. We hugged and hugged. I thought, the woman who has her arms around me is *my* grandmother. Of course I was crying my eyes out.

"Let me take a good look at you," she said. She held me at arms' length and looked me over. Her eyes filled with tears. I thought she was going to say how much I reminded her of my mother. But instead she cried, "Oh, if only my Bill could have seen you!"

She handed me a Kleenex and we both wiped away tears. "I cry so easily," I said.

"Me, too," she said.

We both laughed at that and hugged again.

"Let's pick up your luggage and I'll bring you home," my grandmother said. She sighed. "My, but the old place is so empty without my Bill."

My grandmother seemed lost in thought as we started out on the trip from the airport to the farm. I wanted to ask her questions about my mother, but it didn't seem like the right time. I would be there for two weeks. There'd be plenty of time to talk. So I looked out the window at the landscape instead.

The first thing I noticed about Iowa was that there are no hills or mountains. The sky reaches all the way to the edges of the fields. Iowa — at least where my grandmother lives — is as flat as a pancake. The next thing I noticed about Iowa was that the houses are spread far apart, and that in between the houses are miles and miles of cornfields.

"It's pretty here," I said. "It looks a lot different from where I live."

"Bill used to say, 'Verna, we live in the most beautiful place on the face of the earth.' " She smiled at me, but there were tears in her eyes again. "Your grandfather had a positive attitude and something good to say about everything and everybody," she said. For the rest of the drive to Maynard she described Bill's funeral and shed some more tears.

Finally, she changed the subject. "Here we are in downtown Maynard," she said.

"Where?" I asked. We'd just passed a gas

station and a store and were driving by corn-
fields again.

"That was it," Verna said. "Bill used to say
if you blinked when you drove through Maynard you'd miss it."

I turned and looked out the back window.
There were three other small buildings besides
the gas station and store. "That's the whole
town?" I asked.

"What you see is what you get," she said.
"Remember how your grandpa used to say
that all the time?"

"No," I answered quietly. "I don't remember being here."

In a few minutes we drove up to a big white
farm house. It was surrounded by fields of
corn. "They'll be harvesting the corn over the
next few days," she said. "Bill used to love
harvest time." She sighed. I didn't look, but
I was sure her eyes were filling with tears
again.

"Here we are," she said as she opened the
kitchen door for me to go in. "Home sweet
home."

I walked into a big, friendly looking kitchen.
"It's nice," I said.

"It's terrible not having anyone to cook for,
and eating alone," she said. "I'm glad you're
here."

"Me, too," I said, though I wasn't sure I

meant it. Suddenly I was feeling nervous and shy. As my grandmother showed me around the downstairs of her house, I realized that I didn't feel any special connection with this woman, that my grandmother was a stranger to me. I didn't even feel like calling her "Grandma."

I wondered how I'd feel when I saw my mother's room. I imagined it would be decorated as she'd kept it, with the things she loved best on the walls. Maybe I'd feel more at home in my mother's room.

"Am I staying in my mother's old room?" I asked.

"You're staying in your own room," replied Verna. "But certainly before it was your room, it was hers."

Verna led me upstairs and opened the door to a large room at the end of the hall. "I bet you'll recognize it," she said.

I walked into a sunny room. The walls were pink. There was a big fluffy pink throw rug. Even the bedspread was pink. And instead of posters of rock and roll stars such as the Beatles, the decorations in the room were from nursery rhymes. I couldn't imagine my mother living her teenage years in a room with cutouts of Little Bo Peep, Humpty Dumpty, and Mary with her lamb. Floppy-eared bunnies were painted on the bureau.

"This was my mother's room?" I asked.

"When you came to live with us, Bill insisted that we redecorate for you," she said. "We never bothered to change it. I gave your crib to a neighbor, but otherwise it's the same as it was eleven years ago. Do you remember this room?"

I shook my head.

"I bet the bunnies painted on the bureau look familiar to you," she said. " 'Bun-bun,' was what you called bunnies. Bill was teaching you how to hop like a bunny when your father took you away from us. Do you remember?" Verna looked at me expectantly.

"No," I replied. "I don't remember being here — ever." She looked disappointed. But at the moment I didn't care. I didn't like the way she said that my father took me away from her and Bill. She made it sound as if he'd done something wrong.

"When you've cleaned up, come down for a snack," Verna said. "Then I'll show you the fields and barn. I bet the goats will jog your memory."

But I didn't want to remember living with Verna and Bill. And I didn't want to hear any more about Bill and what he used to say and do. I wanted Verna to tell me about my mother.

While I ate my snack, Verna explained some

of the things she'd planned for us to do together. Most of it revolved around food. She was going to teach me how to bake. And she'd invited three of her closest friends to lunch the next day — which she said I'd help her prepare. "Marion, Ethel, and Janet will remember you," she said. "But I suppose you won't remember them."

"Probably not," I answered. My hands felt clammy. I hated meeting new people. And for the next two weeks everyone I would meet would be a stranger. I felt queasy. I was already homesick and I'd only been in Iowa for two hours.

Verna showed me every inch of the property. She didn't mention my mother once, but kept up a running commentary about what Bill thought of this and what he did about that.

Finally we returned to the house.

"I guess we better get on with the baking," Verna said. She didn't seem very enthusiastic. Neither did I. I hate cooking. Sewing and knitting are fun and interesting to me. But spending a lot of time preparing food is not my idea of a good time. Home economics is the only subject in school that I hated. Well, I thought, maybe when we're cooking Verna will talk about my mother.

In the next few hours we made a chocolate cake, sugar cookies, and prepared a bread dough. But we didn't do much talking. Whenever I asked Verna about my mother she changed the subject. For example, when I said, "Did my mother help you bake, too?" Verna looked at her watch and said, "Two o'clock. Time for my favorite soap opera." She turned on a small kitchen TV and the rest of our baking session was accompanied by my least favorite kind of television — soap operas.

After all that cooking, we still had to prepare our dinner of roast chicken and biscuits. I remembered my mother writing about how wonderful her mother's biscuits were, but I didn't even bother to mention this to Verna.

During dinner Verna was pretty quiet. So was I. I didn't know what to talk to her about. After washing the dinner dishes, I said I was tired and went to my room. I was too disappointed to write letters home. What would I say? "Having a terrible time. Wish I were home."?

The next morning I helped Verna feed the goats. Then we prepared for our luncheon guests. Verna's three friends were nice, but I had absolutely nothing in common with them. They went on for awhile about how beautifully I'd grown up and what a darling baby I'd been, which embarrassed me. Then they gossiped with Verna about who would win what ribbons at the county fair, which bored me. When they were leaving one of the women — Mrs. Baily — took me aside and asked me how I thought my grandmother was doing "after her big loss." I knew she meant Bill's death.

"She talks about him a lot," I answered.

"It's such a blessing that you are here," she said. "See if you can't get her to make up her blackberry jam and enter it in the fair. Will you?"

I nodded.

After our guests were gone, I told Verna I thought it would be neat if she entered her jam in the fair.

"I haven't made it this year," she said. "By the time blackberries were in season, Bill was gone."

"Is it too late to make it now?" I asked.

"I daresay there're still some berries around. Would you like to make it with me?"

"Sure."

"If it's important to you, I guess we could," Verna said.

"I think it'd be fun to go to the fair and see you win a blue ribbon."

Verna's eyes filled with tears. I figured she was thinking about Bill again and all the times he watched her win blue ribbons. I went to my room.

Around five o'clock Verna walked into my room without knocking (something that drives

Nothing went right the night I went to bingo with my grandmother.

me crazy) and said, "Don't forget, we go to bingo in a half hour." She didn't look too happy about going to bingo. I figured it might be the first time she was going since Bill died and was grateful that she didn't say it. Well, maybe bingo will cheer us both up, I thought.

It didn't. I was introduced to all these people who remembered me when I was a baby. They kept saying how nice it was that I was visiting my grandmother "in her time of grief," and how sad my grandparents were when my father took me back.

I hated that evening of bingo and I was

hating being with my grandmother. It was nothing like I thought it would be. We didn't say two words to one another on the way home in the car. I was grumpy and she was sad. We both went to our bedrooms as soon as we arrived home. I wrote a letter to my dad and one to Kristy. But I didn't tell them I was having a terrible time.

The next morning Verna announced that we were going to pick blackberries for the jam. It was a hot muggy day, and blackberry bushes are full of thorns. I could tell that Verna wasn't enjoying the project any more than I was. "Bill used to make this task so much fun," she said. Was she angry at me for *not* making it fun? Was I supposed to be making up for her husband's being dead?

Making jam — at least the way Verna Baker does it — is a long, hot job. The kitchen felt like the inside of a furnace. And Verna kept criticizing the way I did things. When I spilled jam on the counter, she grabbed the pot from me. "I'll finish pouring," she snapped. "You can clean up your mess."

As I reached for the paper towels I heard her mumble under her breath, "It'd be nice if someone said they were sorry."

"Sorry," I said. "But I didn't spill it on purpose. My hands were sweaty and the pot slipped."

"You have to concentrate when you cook. Otherwise there are accidents in the kitchen. What if you'd burned yourself? What do you think your father would do?" She harrumphed. "He'd blame me and never let you come here again, that's what he'd do." I heard her mumble under her breath, again, "We should never have let him take you back."

"Stop criticizing my father," I told her sharply. "I hate when you do that. Besides, I wouldn't have wanted to grow up out here in the middle of nowhere. I wish I'd *never* come here."

I ran out of the kitchen and into the cornfields. I never wanted to see Verna Baker again.

CHAPTER 14

I thought Verna would come running after me. But she didn't. I walked around the corn-fields trying to figure out how I could get home without seeing or talking to her again. But if I wanted to go back to Connecticut I had to tell Verna and my father so they could arrange it. And the sooner I did that, the sooner I'd be on my way. I went back to the house.

I saw Verna before she saw me. She was sitting on the glider couch looking at an opened scrapbook. Tears were pouring down her face. As I came closer it looked as though she were crying over a big school picture of me. Then I saw that it was a photo of my mother when she was around my age. For the first time since I arrived in Iowa, I thought about how I must remind Verna of her own daughter. I thought of how I'd been behaving, and realized that she was probably as disappointed in me as I was in her.

Verna looked up and saw me. "You look so much like Alma," she said. "And you act like her, too — even when you're unhappy about something."

"I'm sorry," I said.

"Oh, child, don't be sorry about being like your mother. It's a blessing for me to see that her life goes on in you. A real blessing. I just wish I could be more helpful to you. I'm so full of sadness right now, because of losing Bill. It's not fair to you. I could understand if you want to go home earlier than we planned."

I stepped onto the porch and sat beside her on the glider. "Do you want me to go home now?" I asked.

"I only want what's good for you," she said.

"That's what my father always says," I told her.

"I've said some terrible things about your father since you've been here. And none of them are fair. I'm sorry."

"I haven't been a very good guest," I admitted.

"It's a difficult situation. In many ways we're strangers to one another."

"My mother is a stranger to me, too," I told her. "I came here to find out more about her. But when I ask questions about her, you change the subject. Also, I'm shy. I hate meet-

My mother working on a project.
I love to sew, too.

ing a lot of new people — and besides cooking, that's all I've done since I've been here."

"Well, my goodness." Verna had stopped crying and seemed very interested in what I was saying and not a bit upset by it. "Tell me more. I want to know everything that's on your mind. What else has bothered you?"

"I hate cooking," I admitted. "I love eating and I think you're a great cook. In a letter my mom wrote me before she died, she said that you were a fabulous cook. And she's right."

"In that letter did she tell you she was a terrible cook herself?" Verna asked.

"No. Was she?"

"She was! Alma loved sewing, knitting, and other handiworks. But she had no talent for cooking."

"I love sewing, too. How else am I like her?"

"I guess I'd have to come to know you better to be able to tell you that," my grandmother said. "Would you like to look at your mother's scrapbook?"

"Will it upset you?"

"I'd like to look at it with you, Mary Anne," she said.

I learned a lot about my mother from her scrapbook. There were report cards (all A's just like me) and a ticket to a Rolling Stones concert. I was just about to ask my grandmother what my mother's favorite children's

Maynard Middle School

Alma Baker, Grade 8
Final grades

	A
Homeroom	A
Math	A
English	A
Science	A
Phys. Ed.	A
Social Science	A
Music	

WBJB
ROCK 'N ROLL
Presents
The
ROLLING
STONES
live in concert
June 24 8 p.m.
Madison Arena
Des Moines, Iowa

Souvenirs from my mother's scrapbook.

books were, when she blurted out, "I have the most wonderful idea!" Her eyes sparkled and she looked happy for the first time since I'd arrived.

"What?" I asked.

"When your mother died, I was working on a quilt as a surprise for her twenty-fifth birthday. It's made up of scraps of cloth I'd saved over the years from things she'd outgrown — like her baby blanket and clothes. There's even a swatch from the fabric we used to make her wedding gown. The quilt was to be something she could pass along to her own child some-day." She paused before going on. "I stopped working on it when she died."

"What's your idea?" I asked in a whisper.

My grandmother took my hand in hers. "I think you should help me finish it. We could both work on it. If we put our minds to it, we could finish it before you go back."

"I'd love to!" I exclaimed. "Oh, Grandma, could we? Could we really?"

"That's the first time you've called me 'Grandma,' " she commented.

"I know," I said. Of course we both started crying again.

Over the ten days that remained of my stay, Grandma and I finished the quilt. I did other things, too. I went on a date with a very boring guy and baby-sat for some neat, but very active, children on a neighboring farm. Grandma did the cooking — all delicious — and I concentrated on the quilt.

The day before I went back East was the first day of the Annual Farm Fair. As we were getting ready to go, I reminded Grandma to bring her blackberry jam for the judging. "I don't think my jam is at its best this year," she said.

"Uh-oh. That's because I helped, isn't it?"

"If you call that help," she joked. "No," she

My grandmother and me in front of our award-winning quilt.

went on, "I think this year I'd like to share a blue ribbon with you. How about we enter Alma's quilt?"

"Yes!" I shouted. "Oh, yes."

I rushed upstairs and brought down the quilt. Grandma said that whether we won the prize or not, the quilt was a winner. A winner for her and me, because it symbolized my mother, and our grandmother-grandaughter relationship.

When I left Iowa the next morning I wondered when I would see my grandmother again. And I felt sad for all the years that I hadn't known her.

When I was back in Stoneybrook I told my father about my trip and how much I loved getting to know my grandmother. He looked concerned. "Do you want to live with Verna?" he asked.

"Dad, no!" I shouted. "You're my *father*. I love you. How could you even think that?"

My father smiled. "I'm glad you're home," he said.

"Me, too."

The following afternoon my grandmother phoned to tell me that we'd won first prize for our quilt. "The next time I see you I'm going to give you the quilt," she said. "But I want to keep that blue ribbon."

I could picture my grandmother alone in her house. I knew she was lonely for her husband, her daughter, and her grandaughter.

"Grandma," I said. "I think you should keep the quilt, too. You did most of it. I just finished it off. Besides, I want you to have it to remember my mother and me."

There was a pause. "Thank you," she said. "You know that it will be yours someday."

"I know," I said softly.

We talked a little bit longer. I told her that my family and friends had met me at the airport. And about the date Logan and I were going to have that night. But there wasn't really much else to say. And I was supposed to be at a Baby-sitters Club meeting. "I'll write you a letter," I promised.

"That would be nice," she said. I could hear the sadness and loneliness in her voice. I looked at the clock. Five-fifteen.

"I have to go to a meeting of that club I told you about," I said.

"Then you better go," she said.

" 'Bye, Grandma."

" 'Bye, Mary Anne."

CHAPTER 15

I finished my autobiography a couple of days before it was due, so I handed it in early. While my friends were working all weekend to finish the stories of their lives, mine was already on Ms. Belcher's desk. I had no one to hang out with. I was glad I had a baby-sitting job at the Rodowskys' on Saturday afternoon.

Thinking about my life so far and writing about it was harder than I thought it would be. It reminded me of how much I missed having a mother. Writing my autobiography also reminded me what a great parent my father is and how well he's raised me on his own. (Except for the year or so that my grand-parents took care of me. I know now that they did a great job, too.)

When I first started to write about the time I failed the vision test at school on purpose, I thought it was a pretty serious story. I used to think of that incident as this terrible thing

I'd done that I'd never tell anyone about. By the time I finished writing that section of my autobiography I realized it was a funny story and that I hadn't committed some awful crime. Sometimes I guess I take myself too seriously. I never told my father I'd failed that test on purpose.

Now I think he'll think it was pretty funny, too. After all, he's the dad who understood that if I was really upset about dancing in public, I shouldn't be in the recital. And he knew how to handle my goof-up when I invited both him and Mimi to the Mother's Day tea party.

Before I left for my baby-sitting job at the Rodowskys', I went to my dad's study and knocked on the door. "You in there, Dad?"

"Yeah, come on in."

He was sitting on the couch, reading the newspaper and looking Saturday-afternoon relaxed. "What's up?" he asked.

"I was wondering if you'd like to read my autobiography when I get it back?"

"Only if you make an A," he teased. My dad is always so worried about hurting my feelings that he immediately added, "That's a joke."

"I know, Dad."

"Well, you always make A's," he said with

a grin, "so I guess I'll have to read it. Are you going to show it to Dawn?"

"Maybe," I replied. "When she comes for Christmas."

The phone rang. "Will you get that?" he asked.

I went to his desk and picked up the phone.

"Hello, Spier-Schafer residence."

"Hello, Spier, this is Schafer," said a cheerful voice on the other end.

"Dawn!" I shrieked. "Dawn, we were just talking about you."

"What'd you say about me?"

"Dad wondered if I wanted you to read my autobiography and I said yes, when you come home for Christmas. Then the phone rang and it's you."

"Mary Anne, this is so creepy," Dawn said. "I mean major creepy. Do you know why I called you?"

"Why?" I asked tentatively. I didn't know if I was going to like the answer. Dawn's voice had dropped to the solemn tone she uses when she talks about ghosts, ESP, and other beyond-the-natural phenomena.

"I called to ask *you* if you wanted to read my autobiography," she said.

"Wow!" I exclaimed. "What a coincidence!"

"It's not a coincidence, Mary Anne. Don't

you see? We read one another's minds. It's ESP."

I didn't have time to debate the question of whether Dawn and I could read one another's minds across three thousand miles. I had to leave for my baby-sitting job. "I've got to go," I said. "I'm sitting for the Rodowskys."

"So, do you want to?"

"Sure," I said. "Do you?"

"I can't wait."

I smiled. I just love the way Dawn and I don't have to complete ideas to understand one another. We both knew we were talking about our autobiographies without having to say it. It's pretty neat having a stepsister, even if she is three thousand miles away.

At the end of English class on Monday everyone else turned in their autobiographies, and Ms. Belcher gave me back mine. "Since you turned it in early, Mary Anne, I thought I'd return the favor." She smiled. "It's such a huge assignment for me to correct, I was glad to have this one early. Thanks."

"Thank you," I said.

The second I was out of the room I leaned against the wall and turned to the back page to see my grade.

STONEYBROOK MIDDLE SCHOOL

J B

A+

Excellent job, Mary Anne! The incidents you chose to write about represent a range of the happy and difficult experiences in your life. You have a talent for writing with emotional honesty and clarity. Your father has done a wonderful job of raising you. But he has a special daughter to care for. **Lucky both of you.**

J. B.

L. GODWIN

Ann M. Martin

About the Author

ANN MATTHEWS MARTIN was born on August 12, 1955. She grew up in Princeton, N.J., with her parents and her younger sister, Jane.

Although Ann used to be a teacher and then an editor of children's books, she's now a full-time writer. She gets the ideas for her books from many different places. Some are based on personal experiences. Others are based on childhood memories and feelings. Many are written about contemporary problems or events.

All of Ann's characters, even the members of the Baby-sitters Club, are made up. (So is Stoneybrook.) But many of her characters are based on real people. Sometimes Ann names her characters after people she knows, other times she chooses names she likes.

In addition to the Baby-sitters Club series, Ann Martin has written many other books for children. Her favorite is *Ten Kids, No Pets* because she loves big families and she loves animals. Her favorite Baby-sitters Club book is *Kristy's Big Day*. (By the way, Kristy is her favorite baby-sitter!)

Ann M. Martin now lives in New York with her cats, Gussie and Woody. Her hobbies are reading, sewing, and needlework — especially making clothes for children.

Read all the books
about **Mary Anne**
in the Baby-sitters Club series
by Ann M. Martin

by Ann M. Martin

❑ MG43388-1 #1	Kristy's Great Idea	$3.50
❑ MG43387-3 #10	Logan Likes Mary Anne!	$3.50
❑ MG43717-8 #15	Little Miss Stoneybrook and Dawn	$3.50
❑ MG43722-4 #20	Kristy and the Walking Disaster	$3.50
❑ MG43347-4 #25	Mary Anne and the Search for Tigger	$3.50
❑ MG42498-X #30	Mary Anne and the Great Romance	$3.50
❑ MG42508-0 #35	Stacey and the Mystery of Stoneybrook	$3.50
❑ MG44082-9 #40	Claudia and the Middle School Mystery	$3.25
❑ MG43574-4 #45	Kristy and the Baby Parade	$3.50
❑ MG44969-9 #50	Dawn's Big Date	$3.50
❑ MG44968-0 #51	Stacey's Ex-Best Friend	$3.50
❑ MG44966-4 #52	Mary Anne + 2 Many Babies	$3.50
❑ MG44967-2 #53	Kristy for President	$3.25
❑ MG44965-6 #54	Mallory and the Dream Horse	$3.25
❑ MG44964-8 #55	Jessi's Gold Medal	$3.25
❑ MG45657-1 #56	Keep Out, Claudia!	$3.50
❑ MG45658-X #57	Dawn Saves the Planet	$3.50
❑ MG45659-8 #58	Stacey's Choice	$3.50
❑ MG45660-1 #59	Mallory Hates Boys (and Gym)	$3.50
❑ MG45662-8 #60	Mary Anne's Makeover	$3.50
❑ MG45663-6 #61	Jessi's and the Awful Secret	$3.50
❑ MG45664-4 #62	Kristy and the Worst Kid Ever	$3.50
❑ MG45665-2 #63	Claudia's Friend	$3.50
❑ MG45666-0 #64	Dawn's Family Feud	$3.50
❑ MG45667-9 #65	Stacey's Big Crush	$3.50
❑ MG47004-3 #66	Maid Mary Anne	$3.50
❑ MG47005-1 #67	Dawn's Big Move	$3.50
❑ MG47006-X #68	Jessi and the Bad Baby-Sitter	$3.50
❑ MG47007-8 #69	Get Well Soon, Mallory!	$3.50
❑ MG47008-6 #70	Stacey and the Cheerleaders	$3.50
❑ MG47009-4 #71	Claudia and the Perfect Boy	$3.50
❑ MG47010-8 #72	Dawn and the We Love Kids Club	$3.50

More titles... ➤

❑ MG47011-6	#73 **Mary Anne and Miss Priss**	$3.50
❑ MG47012-4	#74 **Kristy and the Copycat**	$3.50
❑ MG47013-2	#75 **Jessi's Horrible Prank**	$3.50
❑ MG47014-0	#76 **Stacey's Lie**	$3.50
❑ MG48221-1	#77 **Dawn and Whitney, Friends Forever**	$3.50
❑ MG48222-X	#78 **Claudia and Crazy Peaches**	$3.50
❑ MG48223-8	#79 **Mary Anne Breaks the Rules**	$3.50
❑ MG48224-6	#80 **Mallory Pike, #1 Fan**	$3.50
❑ MG48225-4	#81 **Kristy and Mr. Mom**	$3.50
❑ MG48226-2	#82 **Jessi and the Troublemaker**	$3.50
❑ MG48235-1	#83 **Stacey vs. the BSC**	$3.50
❑ MG48228-9	#84 **Dawn and the School Spirit War**	$3.50
❑ MG48236-X	#85 **Claudi Kishi, Live from WSTO**	$3.50
❑ MG48227-0	#86 **Mary Anne and Camp BSC**	$3.50
❑ MG48237-8	#87 **Stacey and the Bad Girls**	$3.50
❑ MG22872-2	#88 **Farewell, Dawn**	$3.50
❑ MG22873-0	#89 **Kristy and the Dirty Diapers**	$3.50
❑ MG45575-3	**Logan's Story Special Edition Readers' Request**	$3.25
❑ MG47118-X	**Logan Bruno, Boy Baby-sitter** **Special Edition Readers' Request**	$3.50
❑ MG47756-0	**Shannon's Story Special Edition**	$3.50
❑ MG44240-6	**Baby-sitters on Board! Super Special #1**	$3.95
❑ MG44239-2	**Baby-sitters' Summer Vacation Super Special #2**	$3.95
❑ MG43973-1	**Baby-sitters' Winter Vacation Super Special #3**	$3.95
❑ MG42493-9	**Baby-sitters' Island Adventure Super Special #4**	$3.95
❑ MG43575-2	**California Girls! Super Special #5**	$3.95
❑ MG43576-0	**New York, New York! Super Special #6**	$3.95
❑ MG44963-X	**Snowbound Super Special #7**	$3.95
❑ MG44962-X	**Baby-sitters at Shadow Lake Super Special #8**	$3.95
❑ MG45661-X	**Starring the Baby-sitters Club Super Special #9**	$3.95
❑ MG45674-1	**Sea City, Here We Come! Super Special #10**	$3.95
❑ MG47015-9	**The Baby-sitter's Remember Super Special #11**	$3.95
❑ MG48308-0	**Here Come the Bridesmaids Super Special #12**	$3.95

Available wherever you buy books...or use this order form.

Scholastic Inc., P.O. Box 7502, 2931 E. McCarty Street, Jefferson City, MO 65102

Please send me the books I have checked above. I am enclosing $ _____
(please add $2.00 to cover shipping and handling). Send check or money order—no
cash or C.O.D.s please.

Name _____ Birthdate _____

Address _____

City _____ State/Zip _____

Please allow four to six weeks for delivery. Offer good in the U.S. only. Sorry, mail orders are not
available to residents of Canada. Prices subject to change.

Meet the best friends you'll ever have!

by Ann M. Martin

THE BABY-SITTERS CLUB®

by Ann M. Martin

Collect and read these exciting BSC Super Specials, Mysteries, and Super Mysteries along with your favorite Baby-sitters Club books!

BSC Super Specials

BSC Mysteries

More titles ➡

The Baby-sitters Club books continued...

Available wherever you buy books...or use this order form.

Scholastic Inc., P.O. Box 7502, 2931 East McCarty Street, Jefferson City, MO 65102-7502

Please send me the books I have checked above. I am enclosing $ _____
(please add $2.00 to cover shipping and handling). Send check or money order
— no cash or C.O.D.s please.

Name_____ Birthdate_____

Address _____

City_____State/Zip_____

Please allow four to six weeks for delivery. Offer good in the U.S. only. Sorry, mail orders are not
available to residents of Canada. Prices subject to change.

is a Video Club too!

What's the scoop with Dawn, Kristy, Mallory, and the other girls?

Be the first to know with G★I★R★L magazine!

Hey, Baby-sitters Club readers! Now you can be the first on the block to get in on the action of G★I★R★L It's an exciting new magazine that lets you dig in and read...

★ Upcoming selections from Ann Martin's Baby-sitters Club books
★ Fun articles on handling stress, turning dreams into great careers, making and keeping best friends, and much more
★ Plus, all the latest on new movies, books, music, and sports!

To get in on the scoop, just cut and mail this coupon today. And don't forget to tell all your friends about G★I★R★L magazine!

A neat offer for you...6 issues for only $15.00.